I0724081

THE CROWN CITY
REDEMPTION
WORKBOOK PRESS
RECOMMENDED
LITERARY BOOK COMPETITION 2020
L.A. EVANS

WORKBOOK PRESS LLC
187 E Warm Springs Rd,
Suite B285, Las Vegas, NV 89119, USA

Website:        https://workbookpress.com/
Hotline:        1-888-818-4856
Email:          admin@workbookpress.com

Ordering Information:
Quantity sales. Special discounts are available on quantity purchases by corporations, associations, and others.
For details, contact the publisher at the address above.

ISBN-13:        978-1-954753-36-5 (Paperback Version)
                978-1-954753-37-2 (Digital Version)

REV. DATE: 05/03/2021

# *Chapter One*

"Thank God, the ceremony must be over; the ushers just opened the doors," Josh said savoring the last sip of Pinot Noir following dinner at the Japanese restaurant overlooking Crown City's Civic Auditorium. He and his wife, Sam, had been waiting for the ceremony honoring Mr. Chandler as "Man of the Year" to conclude before they separated for the night. "You go take your infernal pictures and I'll head back to the hotel to get some rest," Josh continued.

"Oh you old poop," Sam playfully chided while brandishing her newly purchased digital camera. She was eager to take some more pictures when the celebration was over. "Sure you won't change your mind and come with me?"

"I'm sure. You're driving me crazy with that thing." Josh said through sleepy eyes. "See you back at the hotel." They kissed and separated just outside the restaurant.

Sam hurried to the ground level of the mall, crossed the street and just made it to the front steps of the auditorium as people began pouring out. She snapped the picture of several interesting looking people that attracted her attention. Finally Mr. Chandler came out followed by Sam's new friends Carolyn and Charles who she had met accidentally for the first time just before the ceremony.

Sam worked her way close to them, waved and shouted,

"Hi, it's me again, smile" as she snapped their picture again and again. They waved back and smiled broadly.

"She's a cute kid Charles, too bad she's married," Carolyn said turning to Charles. But before he could respond, Mr. Chandler, just in front of them, stumbled and began to fall, grabbing for other people around him for support. Sam was splattered with droplets of moisture, which she quickly determined to be blood. Someone shouted, "Oh my god, Mr. Chandler has been shot."

Everyone's attention was focused on Mr. Chandler at first, but then Carolyn gasped and clutched her chest. Sam was stunned at the sight of blood oozing around Carolyn's fingers and down the front of her gown. Instinctively she grabbed Carolyn's arm to stop her fall. With Charles' help they slowly lowered Carolyn to the concrete as they both called out her name.

Sam immediately attempted to find a pulse from the carotid artery and to determine if there was any breath sounds. She was covered in blood as she looked at Charles kneeling next to Carolyn's body and cried, "Oh god Mr. Bennington, she's not breathing!" They both stared at Carolyn and each other with disbelief as the paramedics arrived and pushed Sam aside to assessed the severity of Carolyn's injury.

Sam was jostled so much by people trying to help or get a better view, that she moved out of the main crowd and tried to see what was happening from the landing above where Carolyn lay. She stood alone watching until Mr.

Chandler and Carolyn were placed in the ambulance ready to be taken to the hospital.

As he stood by the ambulance Charles caught Sam's eye and raised his hand in recognition and appreciation for her help. Her camera draped uselessly from her arm, as she raised her hand to acknowledge their mutual grief.

What had started out to be a joyous occasion had turned into a nightmare and as Sam stood alone in the darkness and the ambulance disappeared with siren blaring, her mind raced back to why Josh and she had come to Crown City for the weekend.

***

Josh Wolf sat at his computer reviewing the details of a business contract he had just received by Email. Sam, an acronym for the initials of her name, Susanna Alice Martin, sat on the bed surrounded with boxes and wrappings while studying the instructions for the new digital camera that she had just purchased. Josh was nearly forty years old, but most people thought that he and Sam were about the same age even though she was fourteen years his junior. He was ruggedly handsome while she had an all-American tomboy look. Physically they looked like they belonged to the same family; each having sapphire blue eyes and dark brown hair, as if their respective parents had sampled from the same restricted gene pool. His six-foot frame was rectangular and muscular. He looked as if he could "lift a boat", as a friend once said. At about five and a half feet she was slender, firm, graceful and wholesomely attractive. After a thorough review of the email Josh said, "How would you like to take a trip to the coast for a few days?"

"That depends on the reason."

"Some guy is having a private gun sale. He says he has the prototype for the original German Luger. I would really like to have that in my collection. The trip sounds like it could be fun."

"We don't have enough room to display the gun collection you already have, why add to it?"

"This could be a once in a lifetime thing. Besides one of these days we'll have a big house with plenty of room to display the collection."

"Talk is cheap."

"I wouldn't lie to you sweetheart."

"Where is this 'once in a lifetime' thingy?"

"Crown City."

"Isn't that where they have the big parade of flowers and all that hoopla on New Years Day?"

"Yeah, that's the place."

"Maybe I could get some pictures of famous movie stars or something."

"I don't think there are many 'stars' there, but they do put on a great parade. It's the football game where the real action is."

"Who cares about a bunch of ugly old fat guys

deliberately banging into one another?" Sam replied as she snatched a housefly from the air in her hand as it unwisely attempted a fly-by. She held her fist to her ear to confirm his capture. Assured that her cat-like reflexes were still intact, she let her little victim resume his ill-advised adventures.

"You know, it never ceases to amaze me that you're not into sports at all. You are a wonderful athlete and keep yourself in tip-top shape; it's hard to believe that you're not into sports."

"I've told you that mom and dad brought me up to be pretty and smart, not strong and stupid."

"I don't want to get into that argument again. You know perfectly well that there are a lot of athletes who are very smart and who have gone on to excel in non-athletic professions. Hell, we've had senators, governors, and Supreme Court Justices who were jocks, and even you can't call them dumb."

"Yes, I know, and I don't want to go there either. You transformed me from a hundred-pound weakling into a Green Beret fighting machine and I didn't get any dumber I guess." She playfully clenched her fist, bent her arm to display her well-developed biceps and grinned.

"Yeah, we've done a lot together haven't we," Josh wistfully acknowledged. "When I first met you I knew you would be a strong partner able to take care of me when I got old and decrepit. The fact that you were a pretty little thing was a bonus."

"You're just a dirty old man," Sam scolded.

Josh grinned and said, "Back to Crown City. Some guy is going to be honored in a ceremony at the Civic Auditorium next week; my guy wants to display his gun collection during that week and the gun show is right next door to the auditorium in the convention center. That gives us a few days to get organized and travel there. What do you think?"

"Sure, from everything I read it is a beautiful little place. It will give me a chance to try out my new camera. I bet I'll find a star or two. Maybe we could settle down there some day when you retire."

"I wouldn't count on that. In this business you can't retire."

"I can't believe your dad wouldn't let you get out."

"You can believe what you like, but the fact is, I'm in this business till the day I die."

"You talked me into a lot of things while we were in college, but joining 'the family business', as you put it, is not the best decision I ever made."

"I just made you realize that it's ok to express your dark side. You walked into my world voluntarily. Maybe that was the real you all the time and your upbringing just stifled it. For my family and me, it's just a way to make a living. If we didn't do it someone else would."

"I hate when you talk like that."

"Sorry, that's just the way it is. I've done this stuff for

most of my life.  I was raised to believe that what I did was a valued addition to law enforcement.  I went to college to get my union ticket into society, but I have no regrets about my life so far."

"Well I do.  I think immoral behavior is justified only if it's necessary to accomplish a just cause—and only in very special cases at that."

"I think we have a just cause."

"That's just stupid."

"I think you're just being naïve."

"Oh sit on it."

"Now that's real mature," Josh said getting up from the computer.  "I don't want to talk about my profession anymore.  We have a vacation to prepare for.  You make the travel arrangements and I'll pull up some maps."

***

It was dark when they reached Crown City and made their way up "Millionaires Row" on their way to their hotel. Sam suddenly shouted "Stop the car, stop the car!"

"What the hell … what's wrong?"  Josh said as he swung the car to the curb and stopped, while he searched the boulevard for a source of danger.

Without another word, Sam scampered out her door and in one leap, jumped from the ground to the hood of the car and then to the roof.

"What in the hell are you doing?" Josh shouted.

"This street is beautiful. I've just got to get some pictures."

"Oh for Gods sake, are you crazy? You almost gave me a heart attack."

"But just look at these tall palms, magnolias, and the globe streetlights; it's a fairyland. I've got to take this picture; it's better than 'stars'. I need to show mom and dad, they will really like 'em."

"Come down from there, you're going to break your neck or get us arrested."

After taking several shots up and down the street, Sam returned to her seat next to Josh and said, "That was wonderful, you should try that some time, you old foggy."

"We're just lucky a cop didn't come by and put us in jail," Josh huffed as he pulled from the curb and continued to the hotel.

After checking in and unpacking, Josh said, "Let's walk around the Paseo Colorado Mall and Civic Auditorium, I've got to find exactly where my guy is."

"Oh good, I can take some more pictures. The Civic Center and the library are beautiful all lit up like that. I sure hope the pictures turn out; Orange Grove was just gorgeous."

"Yes it was, but you could have been a little more discreet about getting the photos. I would have pulled over and stopped if you had asked in a civilized manner."

"So I'm a little impulsive; big deal."

"Anyway I'm hungry," Josh replied. "Maybe we could find a place to eat after we wander around the place a little bit."

***

On the night of the ceremony Josh and Sam mingled with the crowd entering the auditorium when Josh said, "Let's split up, you wander around and take all the pictures you want; I've got to find the gun collector."

Most of the crowd had entered the auditorium when Sam felt a tap on her shoulder and a good looking "fortyish" stranger, who could pass for Josh's brother, said to her, "I think this belongs to you Ms. Martin." Surprised, she whirled around to see who was addressing her; he presented the rental car contract envelope with her name on it.

"Oh, I'm sorry. I mean, thank you Mr.?"

"Charles Bennington. I just saw you drop it."

"I'm sorry if I seem startled," Sam said as she took a step back to get a better look at Charles. "I'm just visiting and didn't expect someone to be calling out my name."

"I'm sorry if I upset you. But I thought you might need it."

"Well of course, you're very kind, thank you," she said coyly.

"Are you visiting someone in town?"

"Charles, we have to get to our seats," a young woman standing next to Mr. Bennington interrupted.

"Ok Carolyn, but first I'd like you to meet Ms. Martin, she's visiting for a few days."

"Hello Ms. Martin, welcome to Crown City."

"Hello, it's nice to meet you," Sam said as she examined Carolyn up and down. "That is such a beautiful gown; the color goes so well with your eyes."

"Thank you. You seem to be rather casually dressed for the occasion. I envy you, I hate to get all dolled up."

"Me too, but I wasn't invited to the ceremony, I'm just taking pictures with my new digital camera."

"I bet we could get you in if you wanted to," Carolyn suggested.

"That is very sweet, but I think I'll just stay out here and take pictures."

"I was thinking of getting one of those," Carolyn said reaching out for the camera. "This one is so tiny. Can it do everything you want to do with it?"

"It's wonderful. See, it has a three times optical zoom and can take five mega pixel pictures; whatever that means. I can replace these little 'guys' if I want to take a whole bunch of pictures at one time, " Sam said pointing to a tiny flash memory card in the camera.

"The screen is so sharp, it's amazing," Carolyn said as she scanned the crowd with the camera. "Charles you've go to get me one of these."

"The two of you make a lovely couple. Would you mind if I take a picture of you?" Sam asked taking back her camera. "I'd like to have something to remember you by. I'll send you a copy in an email," she promised.

"That would be fun. Give me a hug Charles. We haven't had our picture taken together for a long time."

"That's going to be lovely. Thank you both," Sam said after snapping the picture.

"We'd better get going Charles, we're about the last ones out here."

"You go ahead. Save my seat, I'll be right there."

"Bye Ms. Martin, it was fun meeting you," Carolyn said. "I'll look forward to your e-mail!"

Sam waved as Carolyn walked toward the Auditorium, and said, "I'm sorry Mr. Bennington, I hope I haven't made your wife angry."

"No, no, she's not my wife; I'm not married. That's my sister; she's always in a hurry."

"Oh, that's nice. I mean, I'm glad she's not angry." After a brief pause during which they exchanged admiring glances, Sam said, "There is one other faver you can do me."

"Yes, of course, anything."

"Is that Mr. Chandler getting out of the limo?"

"Why yes, he's with his wife," Charles said disappointedly.

"He must be a wonderful person to be honored like this."

"Well actually he's quite a scoundrel. But I guess every dog deserves a day off the leash."

Sam extended her hand and said, "Thank you Mr. Bennington … for everything."

"The pleasure has been all mine, Ms. Martin." He fumbled in his pocket for a moment, got out a pen and scribbled Carolyn's e-mail address on the back, and then offered his business card to Sam. "Here's Carolyn's e-mail. And if you're in town again, please give me … and Carolyn, a call."

"Thank you. I'll do that." Then reading Charles business card she said, "I'll send the photo in the meantime. Bye."

Sam watched briefly as Charles strode away, then shifted her camera to Mr. Chandler and his wife until Josh joined her. They watched together as Mr. and Mrs. Chandler entered the auditorium.

"I want to take some more pictures, but everybody's gone," Sam frowned. "I feel like I'm on the newspaper of something. Maybe Time Magazine will buy some of them. I could become famous," she said laughing. "Besides I made some new friends tonight."

"Well your friends and everyone else are gone and there's nothing left to take pictures of. Let's go back to the hotel, I'm kind of tired."

"How did the discussion with the mystery man go?"

"It was fine, but time will tell."

"Why don't we grab a quick bite to eat. You can keep me company until the ceremony is over, then you can go back to the hotel and I can take some more pictures."

"Ok, I guess I can live with that."

Josh and Sam entered the Japanese restaurant and were seated. "Oh look at that, you can see right down to the entrance of the auditorium from here," Sam observed.

"I think it would be an even better view from the roof," Josh surmised. "The auditorium is a lovely building at night."

***

Someone shaking her by the shoulders and saying, "Are you alright, are you alright lady," broke her flashback as she stood transfixed in front of the auditorium.

Sam finally responded, "Huh? What?"

"You've been standing there for a long time and you've got blood all over you," the stranger said.

"Oh," she said as she shook her head and then examined the front of her clothes. "I'm fine, the blood's not mine. I tried to help Ms. Bennington, I guess that's where it came from."

"Are you sure you don't need some kind of help," the

Good Samaritan said.

"No. No. I'm fine, really. Thank you for your concern."

"I thought you might need some help. This has been a terrible tragedy. I'm just sick to death."

"Yes I agree. But I'm ok, thank you." Without purpose in her step she sadly trudged back to the hotel and Josh. Upon reaching their hotel room she found him watching television, constantly changing channels. "Josh something terrible happened at the auditorium."

"Oh yeah."

"Mr. Chandler, and Carolyn Bennington were shot."

Josh continued to flip through the channels without answering.

"What are you doing? Didn't you hear me?" Sam asked.

"I'm trying to see if the shooting has reached the newsroom yet."

"But you were already fiddling with the TV when I came in. How did you know about the shooting? I thought you came back to the hotel after we ate."

"Yeah I did."

Neither one spoke as Josh continued to flip through the channels several times before finally the program was interrupted by the breaking news.

"Mr. Winthrop Chandler, a prominent citizen of

Crown City, was shot and killed as he emerged from the Crown City Auditorium following a ceremony in his honor. Apparently the bullet that killed Mr. Chandler also killed Carolyn Bennington, a member of another prominent family in Crown City. Investigation continues at the scene, but at this time we do not know who was responsible for the shooting nor the reason for it. Please stay tuned. We will bring you more information on this terrible event as soon as we have it. We now return to our regularly scheduled program in progress."

"You said you met the girl who was shot?"

"Yes she was with her brother when he returned my rental car envelope that I had dropped. I talked to both of them, I told you. I got splattered with her blood for God's sake. It was horrible."

"Hey, shit happens in a crowd, that's not unusual," Josh responded as he continued to flip channels.

Sam's body went stiff as she slowly sat down on a chair across the room from Josh; anguish scarred her face as she stared at him. After several minutes of intense examination she exclaimed, "My god ... it was you!"

"What are you talking about?"

"You came to Crown City so you could shoot Chandler, didn't you?"

"You should have known."

"The only thing I should have known was that I can't trust you."

"You know what I do."

"You lied to me."

"I'm sorry, but I thought it would be better that way."

"I believed you came to see a gun collector like you said."

"I'm sorry sweetheart. I had hoped you wouldn't find out."

"If I had known in advance I wouldn't have come."

"I know, I'm sorry for deceiving you."

"I met and spoke to her and you shot her," Sam doubled up as if she had been punched in the stomach.

"It was an accident. I shot Chandler and I guess the bullet just went through him."

Sam sat for a few seconds with teary eyes then shouted; "You have just got to get out of this god damn business. It makes me sick!"

"Sometimes I think the same thing, but it can never happen," Josh said as he turned to her. "My god, you've got blood all over you. Did you get hurt?"

"No, but I wish I had." Pointing to the front of her dress she said, "This is from your victims. How does that make you feel?"

"I am so sorry sweetheart. I had no idea you would be so close."

"This is the last straw. I want my normal life back;

with or without you."

"Look I have to go down to Cancun in a couple of weeks to talk to a guy."

"Yeah right, that's what you said about this weekend."

"Honest, it's just talk, nothing else. We can go together, and after I take care of business, we can spend a couple of weeks on the beach, dancing, dining, talking; whatever you like. How does that sound?"

"I'll never be able to forgive you for this. You shot a beautiful young woman who didn't deserve to die. I can't stand to look at you let alone going on vacation with you."

"I said I was sorry, jeez what do you want from me?"

In the early morning, after spending a restless night in separate beds, they silently took a flight back to Chicago where they spent several unhappy days avoiding each other.

# *Chapter Two*

Josh and Sam had reached a flimsy armistice with each other following the Chandler shooting and their flight to Cancun, but neither one of them was happy. "I hope Cancun can bring us a little closer," Josh said as he scanned the scenery from the window of the cab on the way to the hotel.

"The brochure says that Cancun is akin to being in paradise, a perfect mix of nature and culture," Sam said as she read from the brochure. "Amazing beaches, breathtaking water, great shopping and dining, Mayan ruins and cultural riches, world-class hotels, water sports … nothing has been overlooked."

"I came here once before with my parents and I really had a good time," Josh said. Maybe its beauty will make you feel better about me."

"Anything will be better than the fiasco in Crown City. It seemed to be a wonderful town, and I'm disgusted with what you did."

"Yes I know but this could be a turning point for us sweetheart," Josh promised. "I want us to be together forever but we both have to work at it."

"Oh, here we are at the hotel," Sam interjected and as she got out of the cab she turned to Josh and said, "I'll stand here and look pretty while you take care of me."

"Sometimes you doing nothing can be very helpful sweetheart. You make pretty, I'll take care of the luggage."

They registered and then took the elevator to their suite on the eighth floor. They threw their bags on the bed, and before unpacking, Josh made his way to the window. As he looked down at the park he said, "That's where I'm supposed to meet Shorty tomorrow. He wants me to help him with something. I don't anticipate any problems."

Sam joined him at the window and said, "You mean the bench next to the trash barrel?"

"Yeah, charming huh? You can keep an eye on things from here in case there's trouble."

"What do you mean 'trouble'? It's just a talk with a friend isn't it … or is there more to it than what you've told me again?"

"That's all there is to it. But it's always smart to be prepared for the unexpected. Anyway, if something did go wrong you would be safe, that's the only thing that is important to me."

"I want to go with you. You're making me feel uneasy."

"No, I don't want you involved. I'm just going to talk with Shorty. I'll brief you after that. Everything is fine; just get into a vacation frame of mind, ok?"

They finished unpacking, took showers and then went to bed for a mostly restful sleep.

***

In the morning they had breakfast served in bed. While eating Josh said, "You were snoring again last night."

"I was not."

"Yes you were, you must have been in a deep sleep."

"Very loud?"

"No not really, but there was a time when I swear I could detect a melody."

"Oh come on, that doesn't happen."

"At one point I got out of bed to dance to the beautiful music but when the cold air hit my bare fanny I changed my mind."

"You mean the cold room was all that prevented me from waking up to see you naked prancing around the bedroom?"

"Well that and the fact you stopped snoring."

"Really, you come up with the most outrageous things to make fun of me."

"I'm not making fun; I thought it was quite creative actually. It had to be to make me think about getting out of a warm bed and dancing naked in the cold."

"Shame on you for picking on me. But I guess something happened last night, I do have a sore throat."

"There, I rest my case," Josh retorted triumphantly.

About noon Sam said, "You know old man, we have been here for half the day already and we haven't been out to see the sights. What's wrong with us?"

"What do you feel like doing?"

"I don't know, just looking around I guess. Maybe we could go to lunch or sit on the beach."

"I suppose we could go to the movies, or on a sightseeing tour. There's always the beach or something," Josh said without conviction.

"Actually, I'm getting tired just thinking about all the things we could do. I do feel kind of tense though," Sam confided.

"Funny you say that, sweetheart. I don't know if it's tenseness or just lethargy but all I want to do is sit around, read, and be with you."

They smiled at each other and without another word they loafed around the room for the rest of the day, reading and keeping an eye on each other. Just being together, alone, was important.

About eight o'clock Josh prepared to go down and meet Shorty. When the time came they were both anxious to get this "unimportant" meeting out of the way so that they could leave the "Twilight Zone" feeling they had experienced all day.

Sam stood at the window of their room watching the bench where Josh was to meet Shorty. As Josh approached the bench he turned to wave at Sam, and she waved back. He sat there for several minutes, alternately looking at his watch, people, and gazing up at Sam.

Finally, two men wearing long black coats approached from the right. As they reached Josh he looked up and recognized one of them, "Ralph, what are you doing here? I was expecting to see Shorty."

As Josh rose the man he identified as Ralph said, "Hello Josh, I have something for you." Each of the men began to shoot hand guns with silencers concealed beneath their coats. Four shots entered Josh's chest and he crumpled to the ground.

Sam saw the strangers talking to Josh and then saw him crash to the ground. She could not determine the reason but the situation terrified her. The horror of the moment crushed the air out of Sam's lungs forcing her to gasp. Paralyzed, she continued to watch in total horror as the two men gathered Josh's limp body in their arms and dumped him into the trash barrel. A car pulled to the curb in front of the bench; another man raced over and poured a five-gallon can of gasoline into the trash barrel, followed by a lighted match. Flames sprang high into the night air and the three men ran to the car and sped away as a crowd began to form around the inferno. Sam could not breathe throughout the nightmare she witnessed in the park. Finally she became light headed and sank to the floor unconscious.

When she could breathe again, she rose and when she saw the tower or flames she began screaming, "Josh, Oh my God, Josh, Josh," as she pounded on the window in a vain attempt to save him from the raging fire. She continued screaming and pounding until, unable to cope with the horrible event that she had just witnessed; she fell again to the floor unconscious.

When she awoke two hours later, she searched from her window the area where the bench was located, but could see only a few couples casually strolling down the sidewalk. The barrel was gone, the fire was gone and Josh was gone. She began to doubt if what she had seen earlier had really happened. Nevertheless she took the elevator down, and made her way to the bench where Josh had been sitting.

There were only burn marks where the barrel had been. She walked around the bench several times trying to will Joshes return. Finally, accepting that what she had witnessed had really happened and understanding that Josh was dead, her knees weakened and she slowly lowered herself to the bench for support. She sat there for the remainder of the night in an overpowering transcendent state ... oblivious of the cold and unafraid of the curious strangers who passed by. In this tragic condition she acutely felt the pain and emptiness of two deaths, Josh's and her own.

During this period of overwhelming grief she reflected on the repugnant and gruesome reality which had been Josh's "business". She felt first hand the pain and deep emotional torment that can come from murder-for-hire. She emotionally connected the pain of her loss with those of his victims and became overwhelmed with empathy and compassion for the suffering of Josh's victims' families.

***

In the early morning hours she was aroused from her trance by a park security guard that said, "You've been here most of the night. Are you all right?"

Slowly, Sam raised her eyes and said, "Yes, I'm fine."

"Are you sure? You've been here just about all night. What are you waiting for?"

"I'm waiting for my husband. He was to meet me here." She paused for a moment before continuing, "There was a fire here last night, right?"

"Yes, ma'am. Somebody set a trash barrel on fire. I think it was just a few bums trying to keep warm. By the time the fire truck got here, the fire had already burned itself out. There wasn't much left in the barrel, but the police took it away anyway. Did you see the fire?"

Sam stared at the guard for a moment and then said, "Yes I saw it. I think it was my husband."

Puzzled, the guard replied, "Yes ma'am. Have a good day ma'am," and continued his rounds.

Sam sat on the bench for the remainder of the day and into the afternoon hours while people went about their daily lives and birds scrambled to find a bite to eat. In her mind she entered an old time movie theatre that was playing, in black and white, the events of her life from the time she bounced on her father's knee, until the fire that consumed the center of her universe. All the while the computer within her crunched the data in an attempt to bring her to a point of understanding and acceptance. Then the theatre's lights came up and it was time to go outside and face reality.

The stimulus for the awakening was the same guard she had talked to before; he had returned for another shift. This time he asked, "Hello ma'am; are you alright? I guess your husband never showed up, huh?"

Slowly acknowledging the real world she said, "Yes, he was here, but now he's gone."

"If I can be of service, you let me know, ok?" He was again confused by Sam's response but didn't pursue the conversation for fear of where it might go. He had dealt with "crazy" people before and it wasn't pleasant.

"Thank you. I will," Sam assured him.

Finally, as the guard strolled away she told herself that she had to do something other than just sit on the bench the rest of her life. The first thing that came to mind was her father and she dialed her parent's home on her cell. When her father answered, she said, "Daddy … can I come home?"

"Sam, is that you? Is something the matter? Are you all right?"

To which Sam replied, "Yes … Josh has been killed." She was startled to hear the phrase out loud and paused before continuing, "I need to be with you and mom."

"Oh, my God, I am so sorry. What happened?"

"I can't go into details now daddy; it hurts too much." Sam physically felt the pain of her loss and it crushed her voice into gasps.

"Sure, sure sweetheart, no matter what happened you can always come home and stay as long as you want. Let me know when, so I can pick you up. Everything will be ok. I love you sweetheart."

"Bye, daddy. I'll call when I get there."

After talking to her father, Sam mobilized herself, slowly rose and walked back to the hotel. Like an automaton, she packed both Josh's and her bags. She examined the packed bags for several minutes and then hesitantly called Josh's father. "Mr. Wolf, this is Sam. Prepare yourself; I have bad news about Josh."

"What's going on Sam. Is Josh in trouble?"

"Not any more. He was ambushed down here … somebody shot and killed him."

There was silence on the other end of the line and then, "What the hell happened?"

"Josh was to meet Shorty to talk about something. While he was waiting for Shorty to show, a couple of men came up and shot him, and with another guy, burned his remains in a trash barrel."

"God damn it, where in the hell were you when all this happened?"

"I was waiting back in the hotel room. I couldn't do anything about it."

"And I suppose you don't have any idea who is responsible?"

"No, I have no idea."

"Josh said that you told him you wanted out of the business, maybe this is your way of doing that."

"You're trying to blame me, you crazy old fool? Look I'm too upset to deal with your paranoia right now."

"What do you mean you're too upset to deal with things? For gods' sake get a hold of yourself and do something if you're innocent."

"You have the resources to find out who killed Josh; I don't. I'm going home to be with my parents."

"Look, you've been a part of the family for a few years now and I expect you to be more than a sniveling coward."

"I don't want to be a part of the family anymore, the whole thing is disgusting," Sam shouted.

"Over my dead body. If you're too lily-livered to do something, just get your ass out of there. I'll take care of Josh's remains and find out how this happened; I guarantee you that. If it leads to you, you better watch out."

"I had nothing to do with this, you paranoid old bastard." Sam's voice was breaking up as tears raced down her face and into the phone, which was dead on the other end.

Sam quickly finished packing, and took a taxi to the airport.

***

On the plane home she thought about her parents and what they meant to her. Her father had great respect for her as a child and always encouraged her to do and be her best. He often told her that she was "prettier than most women, stronger than most men, and smarter than most everyone." He said that if she could learn to use those characteristics properly, she could attain anything she wanted in life. Sam repeated those words when she began to have self-doubts, and they never failed to bring her the confidence to proceed even if the events of her life became difficult and perplexing. She needed those words now.

Her father always shortened her name to her initials, and she became known to everyone in the family as Sam. He believed that a person's name could create an expectation that helped mold one's character. He thought that the masculine name would make it easier for Sam to live up to his characterization of her.

Sam's father was brilliant. He read everything he could put his hands on and could accurately quote from most of them. However, he was modest in dress and aspirations. The family got by financially on his and her mother's salaries as high school teachers, but they were far from wealthy. Her father would say, "The most important thing in life is character, it defines you throughout your life and is the one aspect for which I wish to be judged, not by how much money I have or my lifestyle." That led to many arguments between her parents that made for Sam a very tense upbringing.

The trappings of wealth fascinated her mother.  She kept up with social events in town … who had money and how they spent it.  She always felt she deserved money and position and carried herself and spoke accordingly. When people met her they instinctively referred to her as Mrs. Martin and always said, "Yes, ma'am."  She had long talks with Sam about her ideas and Sam tried in vain to combine the disparate opinions of her parents into a coherent philosophy of life, which she was never quite able to do.

# *Chapter Three*

After returning to her parent's home Sam said very little and locked herself in her room for a week. She only came out for food and the bathroom.

Finally after her hibernation, Sam descended the stairs and in the kitchen prepared two glasses of iced tea then pushed her way through the screened patio door and said, "Hi daddy, I thought it was time to enter the land of the living again." She set one glass down on the table next to her father and took a seat on the bench beside him.

"Hi sweetheart, it's good to see you out and about. A week is a long time to be cooped up like that. Are you feeling any better?"

"A little I guess, I've been trying to get a better perspective on things."

"It takes time to heal sweetheart, we each have our own way of moving the process along. By the way, you have received a call and several pieces of mail from Mr. Wolf. The number and the mail are on the dining room table."

"I called him from Cancun and he said he would take care of everything dealing with Josh. I'll take a look at the stuff later. Right now I want to spend some time with you."

"Yeah, sometimes I sit here for hours just thinking and

reading. I remember the good times we had taking care of the yard together. I miss your help. It's getting harder and harder to keep up, now that I'm putting on a few years and a few pounds."

"You and the yard will always be beautiful to me pops," Sam said as she put her arm around him.

They sat back in the bench with their arms around each other and quietly enjoyed the afternoon sunshine, letting their minds drift back to the good old days. They said nothing but they communicated just the same.

Finally after several minutes Sam said, "I saw Josh get killed."

"My god Sam you really know how to start a conversation."

Sam looked into her father's eyes for several minutes and then said, "Two guys shot him, threw his dead body in a trash barrel and set it on fire."

"Good lord sweetheart. You saw that?"

"Yeah it's a nightmare I'll never forget."

"I can imagine, that's horrible."

"It was such a shock I passed out."

"Why on earth would someone do that, I mean cold-bloodedly kill someone like that?"

"It's a long story. I didn't tell you everything about Josh. If you know the facts you can better understand the situation."

"I'm all ears, but you don't have to tell me if you're not ready."

"No, it's ok I need to talk about it, I think it will help."

"Yeah, that's what they say."

"When I first met Josh I fell madly in love with him. Looking back I wonder exactly why but when you're young, things just have a special urgency about them I guess."

"That's for sure."

"Shortly after we were married I found out that Josh was a member of an international crime family. They made their money primarily by killing people."

"What?" Mr. Martin said with a startled gasp. "I thought that only happened in the movies."

"It's true."

"And you didn't say anything to me about it?"

"I had trouble acknowledging it to myself and I certainly didn't want anyone else to know."

"Holly mackerel, that's a shocker," Mr. Martin said as he got up and walked back and forth on the porch as he reflected on the situation. "He actually killed people for money?"

"Yeah, and I was married to him. This is the first time I've ever told anyone about it."

"That must have been a difficult thing for you to keep

secret."

"No not really.  It was just too terrible to talk about."

"But after you found out what he did, you still stayed with him?"

"Regrettably yes.  He said that they only accepted contracts on really bad people and in that respect they could be thought of as part of the police department."

"That's stupid."

"I know.  He also said that murder-for-hire was strictly a business—financial gain was the only consideration."

"And you accepted that?"

"Down deep I knew I was just fooling myself, but I was terribly in love with him.  I kept telling myself that I would be able to change him in time."

"That seldom happens."

"For a while there I even accepted the situation and tried not to think about the moral implications.  As time went on and I found out details about the business I became ashamed of staying with him, but I was just too weak to do what needed to be done.  I have been chastising myself ever since for not leaving him while we were still in college."

"I think sometimes people destroy themselves by dwelling too long in the past.  It's best to stay there only long enough to learn from it."  He reached for her and she threw her arms around him and squeezed, holding the embrace until her arms were numb.

Finally Sam pulled away and wiped her eyes with a tissue offered by he father. "Whoa!

That was just what I needed. Thank you for letting me get it off my chest?"

"I does clarify things a little sweetheart. Him being in that kind of business I can better understand the way he died. Man what a terrible situation for you."

At that moment Sam's mother opened the screen door and said, "Dinner is ready. It's time for you to share your daughter with me, dad."

During dinner they talked about what was going on in town and how things had changed since Sam had last been home. During dessert Mrs. Martin said, without prompting, "Daddy said that Josh had been killed."

Sam and her father stared at their plates for an awkward moment before Mr. Martin said, "She told me what happened, mom. I'll tell you about it later, ok?"

"Sure, ok. I just hope they get the bastard who did it. That's all I have to say."

Having nearly finished her meal Sam rose from the table collected her stash of mail and went upstairs to her room to escape further explanations.

***

In the weeks that followed, Sam spent a good deal of time searching her soul trying to determine a course of action that could resolve her emotional turmoil and get her moving again.

Finally, Mr. Martin holding the phone in the family room and calling upstairs said, "Sam there's a call for you it's Mr. Wolf."

"Thank you daddy I'll take it in my room." She picked up the phone, and said, "Ok, I've got it." When she heard her father hang up she said, "Hello Mr. Wolf, how did things go down in Cancun?"

"We got everything taken care of in terms of Josh's body. We decided that no ceremony or wake would be held for Josh because that would just attract attention to the family, and we don't need that."

"Were you able to find out what Shorty had do to with it?"

"We tracked Shorty to his hotel room and he was dead, so that led nowhere."

"I wonder if Josh and Shorty were killed by the same people. Were you able to turn up any evidence in that direction?"

"Not yet but we are working on it. How well did you know Shorty?"

"I didn't know him at all. Why do you ask?"

"You were the last person to see Josh. Maybe Shorty too."

"You crazy old coot, are you implying that I had

something to do with Josh's death again?"

"I ain't implying nothing.  This is serious business and I have to look at all the angles."

"I didn't have anything to do with it; have you got that straight?"

"Why didn't you go down to the park with Josh?"

"This is crazy.  I asked to go but he told me he didn't want me to."

"Did he sound like he expected trouble?"

"No.  If I had thought that I would have gone with him."

"Why didn't you do something to find the killers."

"I told you, I was emotionally overwhelmed.  Besides I didn't know where to start and I thought you could handle it better than me.  You knew more about the details of the trip than I did."

"Well the way you acted sounds kind of fishy to me."

"That's too damn bad.  You had as much to do with the murders as I did.  If you're innocent then I am."

"Don't be stupid. My people are going to continue their investigation in Cancun, and they are going to explore things out in your neck of the woods as well."

"If I find some stranger tailing me, I'll shoot before asking any questions. Just let 'your people' know that."

"That sounds like a declaration of war Sam, are you

sure you want that?"

"All I want is for you to leave me alone. I don't want to have anything to do with you and the 'family'."

"You should have thought about that before marrying my son. I didn't think it was a good idea to begin with, but once you're in you're in until death-do-us-part, if you get my drift."

"Oh I get your drift alright. Screw off you old fart."

"Sounds like war to me Sam; you better watch your back."

Sam shivered with fear and anger as she slammed the phone down. Watching her back would now have to be a full time job.

***

Following Mr. Wolf's disturbing call, Sam tried on several occasions to discuss in more detail her dilemma with her father. During the last of these discussions, Sam said, "Daddy has anyone given you the impression that they were following or watching you the last few days?"

"Can't say that I have, but then I haven't been looking for it. Why do you ask?"

"Oh I don't know, I've gotten on the wrong side of Mr. Wolf and he said he might send some of his people to keep an eye on me."

"Now that you mention it your mom said she felt that she was being watched, but she was vague about it and I thought it was just her being paranoid again."

"Well maybe you should keep an eye out. If you notice anything strange let me know."

"What's his problem?"

"Mr. Wolf accused me of not doing enough to avenge Josh's murder, and we had quite an argument about it. Sometimes I wonder if he might be right. It keeps gnawing at me."

"Well just remember, revenge can often create its own special guilt, so it seldom brings you the peace of mind you're after."

"My emotions are all messed up. When I saw Josh killed I felt a very deep sense of loss but then a sense of freedom. I felt kind of bipolar, I really thought I had lost it."

"So his death was both painful as well as liberating?"

"I really miss him but I think his death released me from his power, his force of will, which was driving me in a direction I knew, deep down, was not right. God that sounds so terrible when I put it into words."

"Love and hate mix in strange ways sometimes. I have read someplace that the loss of a loved one can be felt as a blessing as well as a tragedy."

"I'm not sure I should be telling you all this. There are some things that a child shouldn't tell a parent for fear that they will unjustly share in the guilt; like they failed the child in some way. I don't want you to hurt for something that is strictly my responsibility."

"Sweetheart, I'm an old man, well past the time when I take responsibility for your foibles or for your accomplishments. All I did was plant the seed, you grew into the person you are, with little help from me."

"You had a tremendous effect on me dad. I hate to think what I may have done without the things you taught me."

"Thank you sweetheart, but clearly I could have done better."

"The main thing I have to work on now is getting my emotions under control. I feel that if I had been a stronger person I wouldn't be in the fix that I find myself in."

"You've been through a terrible time sweetheart. Don't be so hard on yourself."

"It's like I gave my identity to Josh and when he died he took it with him. Now I don't know who I really am."

"You can stay here until you find yourself. There's no hurry, I'm sure you'll get a handle on things in time."

"Can you ever forgive me for being such a wimp?"

"Whether I forgive you is of little consequence. You need to forgive yourself; that's what needs to happen."

"Thanks daddy, I know you're right."

"I have confidence that you'll do the right thing. But for heavens' sake don't tell your mother about any of this. It would just kill her."

"No, I wouldn't do that; it was hard enough telling you."

Indicating that he was unable to continue this troublesome discussion, he said, "By the way, mom and I are going out to dinner and catching a movie, how about coming along?"

"Oh I don't think so dad. You and mom go; I'll join you at another time. I need to beat myself up some more before I can be good company."

***

As her parents prepared to leave for the movie Sam said, "Have a nice time you guys, I'll wait up for you." She pulled her father aside and said, "Keep an eye out for curious strangers."

As he got into his car he said, "Ok, it will be fun playing cops and robbers."

"You've got to take this seriously dad."

"Yeah, yeah. I was only joking."

She waved as the car pulled out of the driveway and then she aimlessly wandered about the house and finally sat down with a book to pass the time. Eventually she fell asleep. She was awakened two hours later when the phone rang and she sleepily answered, "Hello, Martin residence."

"This is Officer Collins with the highway patrol. Who am I speaking to?"

"My name is Susanna Martin."

"Are you related to Howard and Florence Martin?"

"Yes, I am their daughter.  What's going on?"

"I'm afraid I have bad news.  Your parents have been in an auto accident."

"Oh, my god," Sam shouted into the phone.

"I'm sorry," Officer Collins said dispassionately. "Your parents are being taken to Methodist Hospital emergency room.  It would be a good idea if you could go down there as soon as possible."

"How serious is it?"

"I encourage you to get down there as soon as you can."

"How did it happen?"

"We're still working on that, but one witness said that your father's car seemed to be racing another car."

"My father racing—you've got to be out of your mind! He's seventy years old."

"Like I said, we're still looking into the details, ma'am."

"Ok, I'm on my way."

Sam was shaking as she arrived at the hospital.  The head nurse who met her said, "I'm sorry Ms. Martin, I'm afraid it's too late.  Your parents were just pronounced dead.  I am terribly sorry."

"I want to see them."

"That is not a good idea Ms. Martin."

Sam screamed, "I said I want to see them," and pushed her way into the ER and pulled back the sheets covering her mother and father. She gasped at the sight of their blood splatters faces.

The officer that accompanied the ambulance to the hospital pulled Sam back into the hallway. She stood silently for a moment with the officer's arm around her and then said, "Officer Collins said on the phone that he thought my father was racing another car. Can you tell me more about that?"

"It was more like he was trying to get away from the other car I think. Your father's car was going too fast for the corner, ran through the guardrail and then into the ravine."

As the officer was finishing his sentence Sam turned and ran down the hall toward the parking lot and drove recklessly to her parents' house. She was convinced that Mr. Wolf had something to do with this and she was afraid for her own safety. She thrust some clothes and other important items into two bags, tossed them into the trunk of her car and drove down several country roads in random directions until she was convinced that she was not followed.

When she determined it was safe she found a payphone and called her Uncle Ernie who was very close to her when she worked with his construction company while she was in high school. "Hello Uncle Ernie, this is Sam."

"Hi Sam; it's been a long time, how are you?"

"I've got really bad news."

"What is it?"

"Both mom and dad were killed in an auto accident tonight."

"Oh my God, that's terrible.  What happened?"

"I don't think it was an accident, and I think that my life may be in danger, too."

"That's preposterous, this isn't gang territory."

"I can't explain things now; I'm afraid out of my wits. The thing is, I can't safely stay here and bury mom and dad.  I desperately need your help."

"I don't understand.  Are you saying you're leaving town and you want me to bury your folks?"

"I know it's a horrible imposition, and if you don't want to do it I will have to stay and do it myself, but I'm not sure I'll live that long."

"Isn't that a bit melodramatic, Sam?"

"Uncle Ernie, I'm really afraid.  I think I'm next."

"Oh my God, you're serious aren't you?"

"I'm terrified, or else I wouldn't have asked such a difficult favor of you.  I know it's hard to believe all this, but I've got to deal with it.  Can you help me?"

"I don't understand all that you're telling me, but if

you need my help you've got it.  What exactly do you want me to do?"

"You are a life saver, Uncle Ernie.  You'll have to go to Mom and Dad's house and find the insurance papers first; I think they are in daddy's desk.  They have plots at Mountain View Cemetery.  If you can sell the house please go ahead; otherwise rent it out.  I'll be back in touch as soon as I can but that won't be for some time.  I'll send you a general power of attorney the first chance I get."

"Ok Sam, I'll do everything I can.  Take care of yourself. Please keep in touch so that I know you're OK and let me know what else I can do."

"Thank you Uncle Ernie I really appreciate this."

"I'll go down to the hospital first thing in the morning after I've found all the insurance papers and whatever at Howard and Florence's house.  Where can I get in touch with you?"

"I'm calling now from a payphone so it can't be traced. I want to keep it that way until things have straightened themselves out.  Use your best judgment taking care of things; I trust you totally.  I'll be in touch as soon as I settle some place and feel that I can safely let you know where I am.  I love you Uncle Ernie."

Sam entered the freeway going north, with no particular destination in mind, just knowing that she had to hide out until she could develop a defense against Mr. Wolf or whoever was after her.

# *Chapter Four*

The Interstate sign to Crown City attracted Sam's attention after she had traveled at high speed for over an hour. It was getting late and she turned in that direction, because she knew her way around town and thought it might be a temporary safe haven.

She took a room in the Huntington Hotel where she registered under the name of Sara A. Mathews. That was the name that she and Josh had chosen for her if 'business' had gone awry and she had to change her identity to become invisible. The false identification known only to the two of them included a new Social Security card and number, birth certificate, drivers' license, credit cards; everything she needed to become Sara A. Mathews—including a childhood history. Her initials remained the same, keeping her nickname and all her initialed clothes and luggage usable.

Her first destination the next morning was the Crown City Main Library and its bank of computers. There she began to compose a poison pill letter to Mr. Wolf, threatening to expose the families' organization if anything happened to her. The letter indicated that she had developed a heavily "firewalled" and multiple password protected web site that contained detailed information disclosing the inner workings of Wolf Enterprises—names, addresses, crimes committed, passwords, account numbers, and security procedures.

If she did not login every forty-eight hours, the contents would be sent directly to the FBI and several Police Departments in cities where the Wolf family had completed contracts. She carefully edited all the information that she had gleaned from Josh's records and her own knowledge. She was convinced that it would be at least temporary a life insurance policy when the Wolf family found her.

It was only after crafting her letter, website and hard copy of the same material, that she was struck with the coincidence of her being drawn to Crown City. It was the location of a most troubling event in her life and a direct precursor to Josh's death. Something brought her here. Maybe in a twisted way it could become the location of her redemption.

Temporarily she put the Wolf family behind her and spent the next two weeks studying maps and books on the history of the city and of its movers and shakers. She reviewed several years of newspapers to become better acquainted with the goings on in society, right up to the death of Mr. Chandler.

Sam spent endless hours reflecting on the fate that brought her to Crown City, and considering her life goals following the loss of Josh and her father who had directed her life until now. She was forced, for the only time in her life, to determine her life goals with no one's input but her own. It was frightening and exhilarating at the same time, but she felt that Crown City was the perfect place to hide out and regenerate.

She frequently fingered the business card of Charles Bennington, debating whether or not to call him. Through her research, she discovered that his family had been in Crown City for five generations. She also learned that the original Mr. Bennington, along with a handful of others, had created this town from acres and acres of orange groves bought with their Eastern earned fortunes. Originally, their intent was to create a winter retreat for themselves and other well to do Midwestern families, but they also recognized that they had a chance to add considerably to their wealth in the process. They bought land cheaply, and alongside the citrus farms they planted, built lavish accommodations for their families. As land values increased, newcomers paid for them by purchasing portions of the pioneers land holdings.

Once the railroad connected Crown City to the rest of the country, the constant inflow of new settlers and the entrepreneurial spirit of the times enabled the original investors to grow their wealth and create a city predominantly occupied by wealthy, cultured, and well educated families whose good taste was soon reflected in vibrant business and cultural institutions designed to meet their special interests. In the early nineteen hundreds Crown City was reported to be the wealthiest city per capita in the US. Now, eighty years later, it had become a prestigious and culturally diverse city of about one hundred and fifty thousand people, blessed with mature tree lined streets and architecturally significant homes, robust businesses and near perfect weather year-round.

Sam drove endlessly around Crown City becoming familiar with the various restaurants and stores. She also searched for the right neighborhood in which she might purchase or rent a house where she would feel comfortable.

She constantly pondered her future, but put off calling Charles Bennington because of the remorse she felt about her part in his sister's death. However, in time she became convinced that talking to him about Carolyn's death might actually reduce her guilt as well as provide her an introduction to Crown City's first families. It was a phone call she had to make.

When she became convinced that she could deal with the potentially highly charged exchange, Sam dialed his number and heard, "Hello, Charles Bennington here."

"Hello, Mr. Bennington, this is Sara Mathews. We met a few months ago at the ceremony honoring Mr. Chandler. You were kind enough to retrieve the car rental contract that I dropped. You said that if I was ever back in town I should give you a call, so here I am."

"Oh, yes, I remember the incident very well, but I seem to remember your name as Ms. Martin."

"Well they both start with an M. What happened after the ceremony was terribly wrenching, that can kind of fog ones memory for unimportant things."

"Well anyway, I certainly remember your face, your camera and your kindness. You were very helpful during those last tragic moments with Carolyn, and I never had an opportunity to thank you properly."

"I think we were both overcome with shock at the time. I am so sorry for the loss of your sister. She was a beautiful young woman. You and your family must still be grieving."

"Yes it has been a tough few months for the family. We have tried to move forward with some success. Carolyn will always be in our hearts."

"I know the pain of losing loved ones first hand," she said with an emotion filled voice as she prepared to share her tragic loss with Charles. "I am sorry to say that my husband and both parents have passed since I was in Crown City."

"Oh my god, you poor kid. Your parents and your husband? I am so sorry."

"The pain was so great that it drove me out of town and dropped me here," tears now spilling over onto her cheeks.

"I'm quite speechless Ms. Mathews. Again, I am so sorry for your loss."

"I felt Carolyn's loss personally, even though I didn't know her well, because I was right there when it happened. Then the added loss of my own family has kind of overwhelmed me."

"Such loses are difficult to deal with alone. Maybe we could get together and help each other through this rough time."

"That sounds like a good idea. By the way, all my friends call me Sam, my initials."

"Yes, of course Sam. Then you should call me Charles."

"Charles it is."

"How long will you be visiting this time?"

"It all depends. If I can find a suitable home to buy, perhaps I may stay."

"What type of home are you looking for?"

"The type is less important than the location. I've been driving around town for a couple of weeks. There are so many lovely areas and homes—I'm baffled."

"Have you been able to find a particular neighborhood you like, or are you still undecided?"

"Confused is a better word. I could use some informed guidance, but I would rather not get involved with a real-estate agent until I have a better feel for the neighborhoods."

"If you can wait until tomorrow, I would love to be your guide. It would also provide an opportunity to get better aquatinted."

"Oh how wonderful. That is such a kind offer."

"Where are you staying?"

"I'm at the Huntington, but I don't want to impose."

"It's no imposition. It can be a great comfort for both of us."

"If you're sure that you can spare the time, I'd be grateful for your help."

"Why don't we meet for breakfast?  We can talk over what you are interested in, get better acquainted, then I'll take you on a tour of Crown City."

"That would be wonderful.  I'll see you in the main dinning room about nine."

"Perfect.  I'll see you then."

Charles, several years older than Sam, had a slim aristocratic face, and the confident bearing befitting his parentage and his respected position in Crown City.  He was about six feet tall, with piercing blue eyes, broad muscular shoulders, small waist and slender hips.  He was known about town as a crafty and accomplished businessman, but someone who was very close to and deeply dependent upon his family.  Upon entering the dinning room, Charles immediately recognized Sam and made his way to her.

"Good morning Sam," he said as he sat down by the window overlooking the flower-laden garden.  "A ringside seat overlooking Paradise; how do you like the Huntington?"

"So far, excellent.  Thank you for coming; how are you?"

"Wonderful, but I'll feel even better after a cup of coffee."

"Good, because I just ordered one for you."

"Thank you, I'm in great need of a wake me up."

"I hoped you wouldn't think it was presumptuous of me. Besides, I can hardly wait to start the tour."

"Good; I thought we could start with the area surrounding this hotel. There are many architecturally significant homes in this neighborhood. Then we could move to the Southwest section of town, which is the oldest and the part I prefer. Are you looking for any particular style or age?"

"I really haven't formed an opinion yet. I'm actually quite flexible about style, but I would prefer an older home I think. Most important is a nice comfortable and safe neighborhood. I can adjust to everything else."

"I don't mean to be crass, but do you have a price range you are shooting for?"

"No, neighborhood is the most important thing. Price is not an issue."

"Good, then we should have a good time. I'm looking forward to spending time with you."

After finishing a small breakfast, Charles said, "Shall we be off?"

"I'll meet you out front in a minute." Sam said eagerly as she made her way to the ladies room.

***

They set about a wide-ranging tour of Crown City. Charles pointed out the many types of houses and explained the virtues of the various neighborhoods while Sam freely expressed her likes and dislikes.

After several hours of touring, Sam said, "I think I prefer the informality of the Craftsman style. I like the natural wood and the way the talent of the artisan is so proudly displayed. Each house feels like a signed painting."

"That's a good choice. Crown City is well known for that style." Then looking at his watch Charles said, "Good lord, look at the time. I'll bet you're starved, I've been very inconsiderate."

"On the contrary, I'm enjoying myself so much that the day has just flown away. I'm sorry that I have taken up almost your entire day."

"Really, it's my pleasure. There is just one more place I would like to show you if you are interested."

"Sure, I can keep going."

"I have to make a phone call first. It will only take a minute." Charles got out of the car and as he walked away he made the call. Upon returning, Charles said, "Ok, it's all set. This time we get to see the inside of the house as well as the outside."

"Wonderful, that will cap a very pleasant day."

"The house is not to far from here and very close to my parents' house. It's a craftsman bungalow in excellent condition. I like it better than my own place."

"Oh, I can hardly wait. It sounds wonderful."

The house was quite different than someone from outside the area would think of when "bungalow" was mentioned. It was not small and it was not "without architectural distinction". It comprised about four thousand square feet of comfortable living space containing naturally stained rare woods elegantly crafted into the stairways, walls and ceilings. The exposed natural woods intricate joinery showcased the unique skills of the craftsmen who built them. Even the uninformed visitors had to appreciate the straightforward yet sophisticated feelings aroused by the care and artistry of the home's quality.

As they pulled into the driveway Sam cataloged its features. Shake roof, shingles painted a light milk chocolate with rust colored window frames and panes, large roof overhang with exposed rafter tails, wide front door with leaded stained glass artfully set in curved flower like frames, a lovely front porch with a small table and two adirondack chairs.

"This is truly charming," Sam exclaimed. "You said we could go in?"

"Sure, let's go." Charles unlocked the beautiful naturally stained oak door, pushed it open with the touch of his finger, and they stepped inside. "The place is completely furnished and the owner will accept either a direct sale or a rent to buy."

As they moved from room to room Sam became more and more enthralled by the house as well as its furnishings. All the polished natural woods and perfectly chosen furnishings shrieked of elegance and good taste. Finally Sam said, "I feel like I belong here. I share the owner's taste without reservation. Where do I sign?"

"That's a big step Sam. You should take some time to think it over."

"There is nothing to think about. When you fall in love, thinking is not relevant."

"I knew you would like it. From the first time I met you I could see a little bit of Carolyn in you."

"What do you mean?" Sam was startled at the mention of Carolyn's name.

"This was Carolyn's home. It's just the way she left it. Nobody has changed a thing since she passed away."

Sam was struck mute, her eyes and mouth open and dry. Finally she gasped, "Oh, Charles, how could you! Please take me back to the hotel."

"I'm sorry Sam. What did I do to upset you?"

Through lowered eyes she said, "Under the circumstances, buying this place is not something I can do."

"But I don't understand, my mother and I thought it was a good idea; a way for the family to move on. It would help us deal with the grief of losing Carolyn. You would be the perfect steward for the house that she loved."

"Charles, I can't talk about it. It's just too personal.

The symbolism staggers me."

"I'm sorry that I sprung it on you like that. Since you never really knew Carolyn, I didn't think that you would object."

"I love the place, but I couldn't deal with moving into Carolyn's house. I would feel too guilty, too unworthy."

"I hoped that you would be the next owner since you seemed like someone who would appreciate it and because of the special nature of our first meeting. The idea was rather comforting for me and the family."

"But you don't know me. You don't know who I am."

"I know that you are a deeply feeling person and I have become fond of you quickly." Charles paused to better consider the situation and then said, "If you like, we could set it up as a rent to buy. That way there would not be a final commitment. Either party could call it quits at any time."

"Right now I'm overwhelmed. I need to go back to the hotel and think this through." Sam said through glassy eyes.

"I apologize for my lack of sensitivity for your feelings, Sam. Your reaction took me quite by surprise. I'm sorry. I'll take you to the hotel. We can talk more tomorrow."

It was a quiet ride to the hotel. Upon arriving Charles opened Sam's door, held her hand and said, "Please think it over Sam. If you really love the place you would be doing my family and me a great favor. Again, I apologize for making you uncomfortable."

"Thank you Charles. I do love the house and everything in it.  The problem is what it means and how I can deal with that."

"Sleep on it tonight, and if you still feel the same way tomorrow, we will forget about it and continue our search elsewhere.  I'll pick you up at nine again.  Is that ok?"

"Yes, maybe after a good nights sleep I will see things differently."

He took her shoulders gently in his hands and kissed her on the cheek.

*** 

At breakfast the next morning Sam said, "I know that you don't understand my reluctance to living in Carolyn's home, but I can't adequately explain it to you right now."

"That's ok Sam, let's make that the final word on it and concentrate on continuing the search."

"Thank you, Charles.  I've decided to concentrate on the Spanish Colonial Revival style.  That's my second favorite.  Yesterday we drove by a Wallace Neff designed house in the same general neighborhood that caught my eye."

"Yes I remember the one. You said you liked it.  I know the listing agent.  I'll introduce you to her and make sure she gives you a good deal.  Let me call her and then I can take you over to the office."

***

Sam finally did purchase the Wallace Neff, moved in, and furnished it under Charles's watchful eye. During this time they saw each other frequently and their mutual fondness grew.

Because she felt partially responsible for Carolyn's death, she was initially reluctant to become romantically involved with Charles. But in time, his charm, money and position won her over. Throughout, she felt guilty about withholding her secret, but knew it was something that she couldn't confess and still maintain their relationship. Besides if people knew of her background she could end up in jail.

During all this time she kept looking over her shoulder for the Wolf family, but there was no contact. She presumed they either lost track of her, or chose not to bother with her. Either way, she was glad they were keeping their distance.

Charles and Sam made an interesting couple. Pleasing to look at, but quite different in temperament. He was calm and studious in his manner, while she was philosophical, impetuous and apt to act with what Charles referred to as "inadequate data".

An engineering experiment, performed several years earlier at a local university, perhaps best described their contrasting personalities. Two robot rats were designed to compete against each other to solve a maze. The first robot, (we'll call him Charles) had tons of on-board logic and memory and was programmed to solve and record the maze step by step as it proceeded methodically. The other robot (Sam) also had a robust memory but was primarily built for speed; it could literally "burn rubber". It was programmed to proceed through the maze almost at random, but at a break neck speed. It was expected to win—not to provide a dialogue as to how it accomplished the feat. When queried at the conclusion of the race, the Charles robot gave a good description of the maze and explained in detail how he solved it. He was startled to find the Sam robot on the podium receiving the winner's trophy. When she was asked the same questions about the maze she simply said, "Who gives a shit, I won." or something to that effect.

# *Chapter Five*

Six months into what became a courtship, Sam and Charles, at the request of Charles' parents, were in his car on their way to afternoon tea at the family home. Sam had just celebrated her birthday the month before and was still aglow with her relationship with Charles. Charles was unaware of Sam's agonizing dilemma about Carolyn's death, or of the danger posed by the Wolf family. However they were constantly on her mind, and she made constant references to guilt, retribution and fear. Charles accepted her philosophical outpourings—even enjoyed them—as part of her captivating personality.

The Benningtons', by inheritance, cunning, and connection still owned a significant proportion of Crown City. Since Sam was a relatively recent relationship for Charles and she was a newcomer to Crown City, his parents only had a few casual meetings with her to this point. Before things progressed too far with their son, they felt it was important for them to assess her suitability as a companion for him. After all, Charles was the Bennington heir, and they could not allow an unworthy opportunist to inveigle herself into their family.

As they entered the front gates of the Bennington estate and started up the long curving drive, flanked by mature California Live Oaks and the old, heavily canopied Moreton Bay Fig, Sam was thrilled at the emerging views of the opulent rambling English manor house. First the six brick chimneys, each with its distinctive Tudor pattern. Then the aged, multicolored slate roof, which created intriguing, images, just as clouds do to poets. The stucco and half-timbered walls spiked the prodigious vegetation that surrounded the home like steeples. The artfully assembled sandstone blocks provided a fortress-like foundation to the magnificent structure. Each time she saw the building she thought it had to be more than just where someone lived; it was just too grand for that. She wondered if people who were born and raised in such homes became accustomed to them as one does with a fragrant rose—until someone comments on its wonderful scent.

Randolph opened the heavy, solid oak door surrounded by the traditional Tudor masonry arch. "Good afternoon Master Charles…Ma'am. Mrs. Bennington asked that I escort you to the side patio where she is waiting."

"Thank you Randolph, it's nice to see you again. Are you well?"

"Yes sir, quite well thank you. Please follow me."

They followed Randolph through the foyer with its grand staircase leading to the second floor. The quarter sawn oak floor was set in a herringbone pattern accented by a border of Honduran mahogany. Several statuary and walnut lined niches punctuated the natural cherry paneled walls. Sam admired the acorn finials and the elaborately carved mahogany balustrades as she passed.

A succession of echoing taps was made when Sam's heals pummeled the floor. She enjoyed the echo of her steps and the rainbow of light generated by the huge crystal chandelier looking down from the middle of a ring of acanthus leaves and thistles making up the rosette on the foyer ceiling.

They made their way through a sitting room where Persian rugs covered a good portion of the oak floors. Elegant linenfold oak paneling surrounded the room. Brass sconces and magnificent Hudson River School oils dotted the walls. Two nail head Italian leather couches provided comfortable seating for visitors to wait for the master of the house.

The sitting room was a shortcut to the small patio where Mrs. Bennington awaited. She rose from her chair and extended her cheek to Charles, and a hand to Sam. "Charles…Ms. Mathews, how lovely to see you. I'm so happy that you were able to join me today. Mr. Bennington will join us shortly; he's cleaning up after his round of golf this morning. Please, have a seat won't you?"

"Hello Mother, thanks for the invitation. Our other meetings left little time for everyone to get well acquainted."

"It's my pleasure Charles." She then turned to Sam and said, "My dear, about your name. Isn't that more of a boy's name?"

"Yes ma'am, I guess it is. My full name is Sara Andre Mathews. Sam is an acronym for it. My father got that started when I was young; it just stuck with me."

"Yes, yes of course.  Would you mind terribly if I refer to you as Sara?"

"No, not at all.  Whatever you like."

"Would you care to join me in a glass of red wine my dear?"

"Thank you, that would be nice."

"You may notice that the label has been removed from the bottle.  It's a little game I play with Randolph.  I try to guess the wine's age and origin just by tasting it.  Of course I'm always right, but he still tries.  He's such a dear.  Will you join me in the game, Sara?"

"Mother, that is hardly fair.  As you say, you're always right."

"Well I know a little about wine, but I don't consider myself to be a wine expert, Mrs. Bennington."

"Yes, of course.  I'll understand if you don't want to play my silly game."

"Actually it sounds kind of fun."

Mrs. Bennington poured three glasses of wine and sat back gleefully anticipating another conquest.  Sam swirled the wine in her glass for a moment as it sat on the table, then raised it to below her nose and sniffed.

"Well what do you think, Sara?"  Mrs. Bennington inquired, anticipating another rapid conquest.

Charles rolled his eyes, "Oh mother, really."

Sam obligingly responded, "It does have a beautiful robust nose; blackcurrants, oak, spice." She then tipped the glass from side to side, "Long legs, full body, yet clear as a priceless Ruby. I'm fairly sure it's French."

Mrs. Bennington could not contain her disappointment with Sam's speculation and she replied with measured agitation. "Yes,dear. Would you say, Bordeaux, Burgundy, Rhone?"

Charles pleaded, "Mother let's just sit back and enjoy the wine. Knowing where it came from and who bottled it won't make it taste any better."

Sam took a small sip of wine and swished it about in her mouth, then took a deep breath before swallowing. "This is outstanding Mrs. Bennington. You are very gracious for sharing it with us."

Mrs. Bennington, becoming eager to demonstrate her wine expertise, said in an irritated voice, "Yes, of course my dear, anyone can tell it's a fine wine. Who was the vintner? What variety is it? What year? Place of origin?" She gesticulated gently with her hands as she spoke.

Adding to Mrs. Bennington's aggravation, Sam took another small sip of wine and performed her previous ritual. Feeling some pressure to provide a more comprehensive analysis, she slowly announced, "Welllll, as I said I don't regard myself to be a wine expert, but I do believe it's a Bordeaux."

Mrs. Bennington frowned and made a small, just noticeable rolling hand motion encouraging Sam to move forward.

Feeling the pressure to continue Sam said, "I think it's a St. Estephe, possibly an 1985 C'os d'Etournel." She paused momentarily, but before Mrs. Bennington could reply, Sam unexpectedly continued. "If I'm not mistaken, Philippe Pechard was the vintner at the time. He retired after that year fearing he would never be able to duplicate such a fine wine. His father Etienne, the vintner before him, died just after the bottling. Some believe that he died with secrets not known to Philippe and that was the real reason he retired. I guess we'll never know for sure. That's my best guess, Mrs. Bennington."

Sam's dialogue was followed by a long pause in the conversation. She sat with the self-assured look of a spelling bee contestant after knowing she had spelled the championship word correctly but before receiving confirmation.

Charles intently watched his mother, ready to pounce to Sam's defense. He didn't have the slightest idea about the accuracy of her response.

Mrs. Bennington sat with a sardonic smile on her face examining the confident—almost smug—look on Sam's face. She mused about the audacity of Sam's crawling so far out on the vine under these circumstances. Finally, she replied, "Quite emphatic my dear, are you quite sure of your verdict?"

"Yes ma'am, St. Estephe, 1985 C'os d'Etournel."

"We won't really know for sure until I read the label

which Randolph placed under the napkin on the wine tray, but I do believe that you are correct about the vintner and year of the wine. I'm impressed, but I must do some reading to confirm the remainder of your story."

"Wonderful, since we both agree, it must be correct. I think that you will find the history to be correct as well. That was fun; I hope we can play more wine games in the future."

"My, you are sure of yourself aren't you, my dear. Let's take a look and see how correct we are." She lifted the bottle and removed the napkin to expose the label and exclaimed, "Yes, just as we suspected....Sam. I think that deserves a toast to both of us."

They all savored the wine and the moment, and then Mrs. Bennington said as she gazed at Sam, "I'm looking forward to introducing you to the rest of the family." They all nodded knowingly and took another sip of wine as Charles' father arrived.

"Sorry I'm so tardy folks. Charles, good to see you as always." He extended his hand, and continued, "Sam this is indeed a pleasure." Sam gripped his hand in her customary manner and Mr. Bennington exclaimed, "My, quite a grip, but please don't squeeze too hard, I need two good hands for golf."

"Don't worry Mr. Bennington, only the bad guys get the 'grip of death'. It's a pleasure to see you again."

"Hi sweetheart, have you been entertaining Sam with your wine game?"

Mrs. Bennington, with a slight smile on her face, just blinked her eyes and nodded.

"Has Charles told you Sam, she is always right. No one has beaten her yet."

"It was fun, and she remains the champ," Sam responded. Knowing that those words would please Mrs. Bennington, she made eye contact and gave a wee smile.

"Besides wine, what else were you discussing?" Mr. Bennington inquired.

"Well nothing really, we were just getting settled in, Dad. Sam and I are going downtown later to see the Chandler Building and decide if we'd like to make a bid for it. I must confess that Sam is more excited about it than I am. It will require a lot of refurbishing, and it does belong to Mrs. Chandler." Charles had a smirk on his face and a derisive tone when he said "Chandler".

Mr. Bennington broke in; "I love that building. Uncovering and restoring that old lady's face would be a worthwhile effort. If I were younger I'd jump at it; assuming the price was right of course. I wanted to buy the building years ago, but that scoundrel Chandler stole it right out from under me. That son-of-a-gun probably shed his skin annually and ate small rodents whole. I never liked that snake in the grass."

"I understand there has been bad blood between your two families. Wasn't Mr. Chandler the one who was shot last year?" Sam probed.

"Yes, he's the one."

"Did anyone ever figure out who did the shooting and why?"

"No. I guess it's still an open case, but I don't think anyone has pursued it in a while, and that's fine with me. What about the building?"

Mr. Bennington clearly wanted to change the subject, so Sam demurred. "Mrs. Chandler is only asking ten mil and I think with another two or three we can convert the old lady to professional suites, offices, retail space and possibly apartments on the top three floors if we can get it permitted. This would provide a consistent cash flow for years."

"That does sound reasonable." Mr. Bennington mused.

"You can't find another building in town with the distinctive character of that one," Sam continued. "It blends the neo classical and baroque styles so skillfully that I feel like everything about it is unique. I think the upper echelon professionals will be looking for that. If we do it right, we should be able to double or triple our money in five years."

"How do you intend to finance the deal?"

"Well I feel so confident that I would be willing to put up half the necessary cash myself. Charles must decide what would work best for him."

"Do you have someone in mind to do the restoration and remodeling?"

"I want to take an active role in the design and restoration, and perhaps work with William Ellis, the restoration architect who did the Bradford building. I'm excited about it."

"I can see that, but I get tired just thinking about the effort that will take. Are you sure you're up to it?"

"I have a degree in architecture with an economics minor, though I've never practiced. My Uncle Ernie owns a small construction company where I worked summers. I don't mind getting my hands dirty. If we were to go with Uncle Ernie's company, we could control all aspects of the deal so that everything is done just right. Right now I have the time to devote to something that I enjoy, so I know I can do it."

"Don't underestimate her Charles. If she knows as much about architecture as she knows about wine I would have to be in her corner," Mrs. Bennington broke in; returning Sam's previously given compliment. She had a glimmer of admiration on her face as she spoke.

"Ok, but still that's a lot of money to tie up in one deal. Are you sure you have adequate funds to do this and still have the needed liquidity?"

"Sure, but even if the deal sours, I would be just fine. I need some losses to offset gains on other investments. I'm not worried either way." Sam paused and then, "Say something Charles; I feel like I'm monopolizing the conversation. How do you feel about it?"

"Well it sounds ok, I guess. I probably wouldn't have

much to do with the actual remodeling. It would be mostly your baby. We can discuss it more on the way down town to see the Building. Maybe we should get going?"

Before Sam could respond Mr. Bennington interrupted, "But before you leave can you tell us a little more about yourself Sam."

"There's not much to tell."

"Just humor an old goat; where are you from, what's your educational background; that sort of thing?"

"I was born and raised about a hundred miles South of here. My mother and father were both high school teachers and gave me a good education. They also taught me the value of money. I went to college on scholarships, married a man about fourteen years my senior who had just returned to college after working in his family business for several years."

"What was the family business," inquired Mr. Bennington.

"Real-estate investment and property management, primarily," Sam said guardedly.

"Sounds very similar to ours, or I should say to Charles', since he is doing most of the investing now. I just sit back and enjoy life. What happened to your husband if you don't mind my asking."

Sam chose her words carefully and tried not to become tearful—as often happened when she recalled this painful period of her life. "We were very happy for the time we had together. Not long after we graduated, Josh was killed in an accident while hunting. It was a short time after Mr. Chandler was killed, I believe. His death swept over me like an avalanche. I felt like I was buried alive. I moved back with my parents for a while in order to get my feet back on the ground."

"Good lord Sam, if I had known I wouldn't have asked. Charles, you should have told us."

"That's ok Mr. Bennington, time is a determined healer. The worst part was that while I was recovering, both of my parents were killed in an auto accident." She paused briefly to control the emotional lump in her throat and the slight moisture in her eyes, before continuing. "Because I had gained strength while with them, I was better able to deal with their passing than I was when my husband died. After my parents died, I felt it was best to go some place else—just too many memories. I moved here to start over, one more time. I hope the third time will provide a lifetime less filled with tragedies. I'm on the right track I think. Josh left me pretty well fixed financially, and my investments since his death have been quite successful."

"Oh my dear such a sad story. I do hope that Crown City will provide the nourishment you need." Mrs. Bennington said sympathetically.

"Yes, since I settled here and met Charles, things are becoming much better. But Charles is right; I guess it is about time we got downtown." She rose and said,

"Goodbye, Mr. Bennington."   After shaking his hand she approached Mrs. Bennington and said, "Thank you for the wine and the very pleasant afternoon, Mrs. Bennington."

"It was a pleasure dear. Remember the family is getting together at the club on Saturday. We expect you to be there. In the meantime I'll be checking up on Philippe Pechard." Her ingratiating tone surprised and pleased the two Charles'.

"Bye Father, Mother; we'll let ourselves out. See you Saturday evening."

***

"That seemed to go well, don't you think Sam?" Charles said as he and Sam drove toward town.

"Yes, I think it did; although your father seemed a bit concerned about a few things."

"Yes, he likes to dot all the I's. But he seemed as impressed with you as he does about anything. I could tell that mother was really smitten. I've never seen her warm up so quickly to someone."

"I guess all you need to know is a little bit about wine." Sam opined.

"A little bit. That's quite an understatement. I think mother was literally stunned by the history lesson. I've never seen her speechless before."

"It was fun," Sam smiled.

On the way to town Sam thought about the gathering that Mr. and Mrs. Bennington had arranged for Saturday at the country club. The group would consist of Bennington family members and friends who literally ran Crown City. It was going to be a long intense night of introductions and auditions. She was willing to undergo the trauma because it was a necessary step in her effort to establish herself as a bona-fide member of the community. It was also going to help her better understand herself and her future.

# *Chapter Six*

It was Saturday afternoon and Sam turned the water off, opened the shower door and wrapped a large fluffy towel about her bronze, chiseled body. She then used a small towel to ruffle her hair, which required only towel drying to enchantingly accent her high cheekbones, large luminous blue eyes, and full pouting lips.

Sam spent some time examining herself in the mirror as she struck several poses, which displayed to advantage her pleasing figure. Long hours working out, running, and playing tennis had created a look befitting a national fitness contest winner. She admired her translucent skin and firm muscle tone in the mirror as her movements accentuated smooth yet well defined muscle groups in her arms and legs. "Washboard abs" created a solid foundation for her firm and well rounded breasts with nipples standing at attention like little soldiers.

She wrapped herself in a towel and sauntered to the window where she admired another in a string of bright sunny and cloudless days. The carefully selected placement of California Live Oaks, Pitosporum and her favorite, Jacaranda, stood like centurions guarding the expansive grounds surrounding her handsome Spanish Colonial Revival home.

Satisfaction was the predominant mood as her mind drifted back to how she first met and fell in love with Josh. The real story was a little different than the one she had told Charles' parents. After falling hopelessly in love and marrying Josh shortly after enrolling in college, she was startled to learn that the family construction and real estate business he at first told her about was a front for a murder-for-hire enterprise. She was appalled when she learned of his true background and she left him. But they were enrolled in several of the same classes, and inevitably they saw each other in class and around campus. He was overwhelmingly persistent in his pursuit of her and eventually, trapped by their mutually strong physical attraction, and her unwavering belief that she could change him, she gradually relented, and moved back in. The marriage bond held her fast as slowly he coaxed her toward his hedonistic belief system and she eventually became ensnarled into his unsavory "business" by her tacit tolerance of his lifestyle.

A feeling of sadness and despair swept over her as she recalled the real story that Charles and his parents would never hear from her lips.

As she continued to gaze out the window, it occurred to her that she wanted to take a bottle of champagne to Hector, a valet at the Club whose wife had just given birth to a baby boy. She hastily donned a sheer cover up, descended the stairs and went to the refrigerator in the pool house where she stored the champagne.

While removing the bottle from the refrigerator she heard a familiar voice from behind her, "Buenos dias Senora Mathews, you look magnifico. You come for your love from me?" It was Ramon, with his Mr. Universe like body, stripped to the waist as he usually was while cleaning the pool.

Startled, Sam didn't comprehend Ramon's words and responded, "Ramon, you scared me, I didn't know anyone was here. I was just getting a bottle of champagne for tonight."

"Yeah sure, you don't need pretend. I know you come for a love just like other ladies in these houses. Here, I have something big and hard for you. I let you hold it."

"Why you disgusting idiot. Are you drunk?" Sam responded, as she became fully aware of his words and intent. "You may have other ladies in the neighborhood, but you're out of luck here. Now get out of my way. I'm going back in the house."

"I know you want it missy, no need pretend. Look how you dress. Grasping his crotch, Ramon advanced toward her saying, "I have what you came for."

"Ramon, as far as I'm concerned, you clean the pool and that's it. Now just move aside and let me out, or I'll smash your face with this bottle."

"Ha, ha, you play hard to get with me missy, I like that. I give you what you really want."

When her came for her, she tripped as she backed away, then fell to the couch loosing her grip on the bottle. She was able to fight him off by getting her feet in his stomach and pushing as hard as she could, sending him careening across the room. "Get away from me you disgusting fool."

"Oh, baby this gonna be fun. Fightin' make me bigger and better."

As he came for her again she grabbed the bottle, turned and swung it on an upward arc with all the strength she had. The force of the blow caused a sickening sound as it crashed against the left side of Ramon's face, forcing him to a standing position. He took three steps backward, trying to regain his balance all the while staring at Sam with vacant eyes. Color drained from his face and his legs failed to support him as he slithered to the floor like discarded apparel.

Ramon's distorted face and crumpled body stirred in Sam a cauldron of emotions as she reached down to see if she could detect a pulse. Unable to find one, she exclaimed "Oh my god what have I done? What have I done?"

After pondering for a moment, she reached for the phone. As she picked it up, she found herself in a savage moral struggle. Calling 911 was the right thing to do, but if she did, it could ruin everything she had been working for since moving to Crown City. She thrashed the moral dilemma about in her mind. Conflicted, she laid the phone down and stared at the lifeless form lying on the floor, silently debating the best thing for her to do.

The Bennington family would not accept a scandalous confrontation like this. The way she was dressed, nobody would believe her story. They would think she was just like some of the sex-starved housewives on Ramon's route.

As time passed, the indoctrination she had received from Josh over the years took over. That's what had worked for her in the past with messy situations. Self-preservation became controlling. Morality-be-damned, her future was at stake and she had to do whatever it took not to be associated with Ramon's death.

Before blood reached the floor, Sam dragged Ramon's limp body to the side of the pool containing the diving board. She adjusted his watch to read one hour ahead and smashed it against the deck coping, causing it to stop. Raising the body to a near standing position she pushed Ramon in such a way that the crushed portion of his face struck the edge of the coping before splashing into the pool. Like a water saturated leaf, his lifeless body sank aimlessly toward the bottom of the pool.

Sam carefully examined the pool house and the area around the pool as if it were a crime scene, eliminating any evidence that she had been present during Ramon's "accident". Her past conditioning controlled her: cool calculating and without emotion. No one had seen what happened; with proper care she may be able to get out of this without taking responsibility.

She arranged the pool chemicals and equipment in such a way that a quick investigation might suggest that Ramon had tripped, and hit his head as he fell into the pool. No time to do much else. She never looked at the pool as she retrieved the bottle of Champagne, shut the door of the pool house and hurried upstairs to ready herself for dinner.

While getting dressed and gift-wrapping the bottle of Champagne; she attempted to think of nothing besides the upcoming Bennington family get together—as if the pool house catastrophe had not occurred. She attempted to "will" the horrible episode to evaporate. Josh had taught her to disconnect bad events from the real world and continue as if they had not occurred; it was just business.

However, as hard as she struggled, images of what had happened at the pool house eventually overwhelmed her. Questions about how she had reacted flooded her mind and she thought, "Why did I try to cover it up? Why didn't I call for an ambulance? What kind of person am I? Will I ever be free of Josh? Before today I was convinced that my father's teaching had replaced Josh's. Do two different personalities inhabit this body?"

Considering the events that had taken place in the pool house, she was faced with a dilemma. How could a wealthy person of good moral character kill a man, attempt to conceal it, and then get dressed and drive to a party as if nothing of consequence had happened? Into the rabbit hole and out.

She tried to tell herself that—while suggestive—character is an imprecise predictor of behavior. Individuals are neither as pure as the water in a crystal clear mountain spring, nor as putrid as untreated sewer sludge. Circumstances and the emotional reaction to them can at times overwhelm a person of generally good moral character and cause them to perform antisocial acts.

But no one is constantly as the casual observer perceives him or her, or perhaps as they see themselves after performing one particular action. The accumulation of actions determines a person's placement on the character continuum, and history retroactively records ones' character. Sam felt her actions placed her precariously straddling the fulcrum at the moment.

# *Chapter Seven*

Driving her XK8, hair flying in the wind, Sam entered the long driveway to the Country Club, which was lined with arching Camphor trees, creating a variegated umbrella for the roadway. She pulled to a stop in front of the valet.

Sam was still preoccupied by the paradox of the character continuum, but nevertheless presented a calm and peaceful exterior demeanor. Hector, the valet captain, always came for Sam's car no matter what he was doing. "Hello Hector, I knew I would see you today. I brought you a bottle of champagne so you and your wife can celebrate the new baby. When will she be coming home?"

"Good evening Ms. Mathews, it's a pleasure to see you. My wife is home now. She said to thank you for the card you sent—so thank you for the card. We'll celebrate tomorrow with this champagne. Thanks for everything."

"Don't mention it Hector, I appreciate your good care. By the way, what time is it? I have trouble reading my new watch."

"It's fifteen past six, Ms. Mathews." He paused. "That's early for you."

Sam acknowledged the time as she headed for the Clubhouse. The unusual building reflected the diverse tastes of the early Crown City settlers who had it built.

Among them, of course, was the first Charles Bennington.

There were two separate entrances. The one, from a side parking lot was rather modern, with huge glass windows displaying golf and tennis equipment for sale. The entrance door led to a display area, past the pro shop and the reservation counter, and subsequently to a casual dinning terrace overlooking the tennis courts, swimming pool, and reflecting pool fountain.

The entrance from the front parking lot was completely different, intended to create a grand reception area for business meetings and social events. For this entrance, the original founders had imported the facade of a sixteenth century English Abbey. It featured thick sandstone walls with arched leaded glass windows on each side of the entryway. A steeply pitched, triangular roof covered with aged slate topped the entryway's marble steps. Prominent columns on either side of the steps supported the roof. The original abbey door was twelve feet tall and surrounded by ever wider and taller ornamental concrete arches. The arches channeled one's approach to the, solid oak door with an enormous hammered iron knocker and door handle.

Sam went up the stairs and into the lobby. People at the door simply waved as they recognized a friend and a frequent visitor.

Upon entry, the thirty by thirty-foot lobby was restful and dignified, with Carrara marble floors. The paneled walls and the coffered ceiling were all taken from the same Abbey that had provided the façade and front door.

In the center of the lobby was an antique Parson's table over which hung an elegant Murano glass chandelier.

The wall opposite the door housed a small bar, to the left of that was the entrance to the formal dinning area. The kitchen was directly behind the small bar. To the right of the entry door was a courtesy desk and the entrance to the administrative offices. To the immediate left were two nail-head leather couches, side tables on which sat lamps complimenting the chandelier, and a coffee table resembling the Parsons table. Charles rose from one of the couches where he was conversing with friends and came to meet Sam.

"Hi CB, sorry we had to meet like this. I was tied up until the last minute."

They embraced and Charles said, "Why are you going all formal on me?" CB was what many of Charles' friends called him. Some friends even went so far as to call him CB3 or simply "Trip" after his full name, Charles Agustus Bennington III.

"Oh, I don't know, you look so handsome and distinguished; it just seemed to be the thing to do."

Charles smiled as they moved through the lobby together. Sam could not resist noticing the usual suspects in the club dinning room—the domineering wife (husband), the submissive wife (husband), couples with rumored affairs, and especially women reputed to have had affairs with Ramon. The thought flashed through her mind that some of the women would be very horny in the weeks to come, and she smiled at the sick humor.

A few couples were scattered throughout the crowd that seemed to be happily married. There weren't many of those.

They made their way down the paneled hallway on the right side of the building, which led to a series of five meeting rooms named for each of the original financial backers. Each door came from the Abbey. Stenciled over each door in gold script was the name of the donor for that room. At the end of the hall was a uniquely carved mahogany door with "Bennington" in gold lettering over it. This, the largest of the named rooms, was Charles' and Sam's destination for the evening.

Two walls of glass with vistas of the golf course, including the eighteenth green, comprised the two sides of the room.

About twenty people had gathered around the table by the time that Charles and Sam entered the Bennington room. After they had taken their seats and were settled in, Charles' father stood at the head of the table and lightly struck his knife to the side of his wineglass. "Family and friends, thank you for coming tonight. Veronica and I have asked you here to meet a very special person in Charles' life, so I'll turn the time over to him to make the introduction--Charles." Applause.

"Thank you father. Ms. Sara Andre Mathews, better known to friends as Sam, has become very important to me since we first met about a year ago. I hope you will get to know her as well. Knowing her will brighten your life as it has mine." He briefly paused as he fondly gazed down at Sam. "Before I get long winded, I would like to introduce Sam to those who have not met her and allow her to say a few words--Sam." Applause.

"Thank you Charles and Mr. and Mrs. Bennington, I appreciate your many, but probably undeserved, compliments and will attempt to live up to them as best I can. My complexion is usually not so flushed-- kind words bring color to my cheeks." She paused and nodded toward Mr. and Mrs. Bennington. "I have learned that Mr. Bennington does not bestow invitations to gatherings lightly. His invitees must be of great merit as well as character, so I feel honored to be among you. I am looking forward to getting to know each of you, and am sure that I'm going to have an interesting and productive future in this wonderful city."

Sam turned to Mr. Bennington; he smiled, rose and said, "Glad to have you with us, Sam. Now everyone please start eating before dinner gets cold." Applause.

After dinner, Charles and Sam made their way around the table making introductions and small talk as they went.

When all the guests had departed, Sam and Charles strolled onto the patio where a slight breeze had started to cool the evening.

"You know Sam; I think I'm falling in love with you."

"Oh no, that would be terrible. That could really complicate our lives."

"I know, but I can't help myself."

Sam smiled and after a pause said, "Yes, things are going so well right now that it's kind of spooky." Their kiss was followed by silence.

Sam gazed around the club grounds, then focused on the reflecting pool fountain that always fascinated her. It had several nozzles spouting water in high arcs from the edge of the pool into its center. The scene—to her—was a metaphor for life. The water in the pool was the "sea of life" composed of life's sustaining elements. The water coming from the nozzles was the beginning of an individual life. The stream's arc was that person's lifetime. The rise represented growth and development. The zenith was midlife and fulfillment of individual aspirations. The decline was enjoying what had been accomplished, followed by aging and returning the individual to the sea of life. There, all the person's elements were scattered and mixed randomly with those of others, ready to give birth to another individual.

"Sam you look very deep in thought, is there something troubling you?"

"Oh I don't know CB, do you ever think about the four W's of life; Who am I? Where did I come from? Why am I here? Where am I going?"

"Can't say that I've given it much thought, other than on Sundays. I'm pretty conventional in that regard."

"Yeah, I guess most of the people here are."

"Those are interesting questions, but then I'm a simple man with a simple agenda. I come from a long line of

Benningtons and my values sort of grew from them."

"My daddy always taught me to treat other people the way I like be treated and to live each day as if it was going to be my last," Sam confided.

"That's very admiral my dear."

"Yeah, but then I went away to college and Josh led me away from that, into more of an aggressive, hedonistic point of view. Now I have lost both my father and Josh and I'm trying to formulate a philosophy that is somewhere in between, and all my own."

"I'm a good Episcopalian, so maybe I've at least got a start," Charles said proudly.

"I've always had trouble buying into most of the constructs and ceremony of organized religion," Sam smiled at the simplicity of Charles remark. "I believe that religious groups have always done a great deal of social good, and I don't want to minimize that. But in order to acquire the necessary resources for that, over time, they generally develop authoritarian belief systems that coerce people to follow their particular dogma and ritual."

"But that sounds like a small price to pay for the social and educational services that religious groups provide," Charles reasoned. "After all, the ritual and ceremony are only there as a reminder that you should live the good life much like the early founders of the churches did."

"The problem arises because religious systems are not content to simply state their beliefs and let people make up their own minds," Sam countered. "They are afraid that if they give people too much freedom, it would result in an uncertain future for the organization."

"That could very well be true. For many people, meeting their life's sustaining needs is difficult, without setting aside money for Church charities. They may be too short sighted without a religious kick in the pants," Charles said with a clenched jaw. "Maintaining the churches' good works takes money, but that is less expensive than welfare services provided by civil government."

"I think you're selling people short Charles. Most people give to charity willingly without subjecting themselves to the dishonest nature of religious systems and the damage they do."

"What do you mean by that?" Charles inquired. "You just said that religious groups do a lot of good charity works. And I believe they also provide people a stability that makes their lives happier; particularly in the face of tragic events."

"I can't argue with that, but the rigidity and ceremony of a religious system, teaching as they do, that they have a unique connection to God, ultimately collides with other rigid systems that have different beliefs. Rather than help people put order into an apparent haphazard existence, they cause conflict between otherwise peaceful people. History has shown that to be consistently the case."

Charles countered, "The best religious systems are reasonably tolerant, though when they get mixed up with the political system there can be trouble."

"But the exception seems to keep proving the rule. If religion were our only source of knowledge, we would still believe that the Earth was the center of the universe."

"Now you're just picking one outrageous example. During the dark ages the church was a major contributor to the knowledge base of the time. Without it, we may still be in the dark ages."

"When looked at logically, religious systems all seem contrived; obviously designed to keep people in line and obligated to a central authority in order to guarantee donations which keep the house of cards afloat. Unfortunately, the people that run them are so biased that they often don't keep the best interest of the people they serve in mind."

"You can say the same thing about many civil governments. You have a very hostile view of religion Sam; it surprises me. But you do believe in God, don't you?"

"Well in my own personal way."

"What do you mean? God is God. How else can you explain the orderliness of the Universe?"

"Well, God to me is a hypothetical construct devised by men to help explain the unknown and possibly the unknowable. To say you believe in God is to say you believe in a concept, which is unknowable. Belief must trump reason, which is what faith is. That seems to be ok for most people, but I think that faith without facts is folly."

"If you can come up with a better explanation for the orderliness in the universe, I'd like to hear it."

"First you have to explain the origin of God. Then I can use the same explanation for the origin and orderliness of the universe. One is as difficult to explain as the other, but most people take the existence of God for granted. Now it may be true that there is an unseen power that directs the major operation of the universe."

"Yes of course, that's the way it is," Charles interrupted.

"Nobody really knows about that, though I do believe that if that Power does exist, it only affects individuals in a remote way. It doesn't watch over them, listen to their prayers, and intercede in their lives in any meaningful way. That's a pipe dream that religious systems broadcast to keep people locked into the system."

"Hmm, now you're beginning to lose me. I don't know how you could believe there is a power wise and strong enough to run an orderly universe, and yet not wise enough to intercede in an individual's life."

"It is only orderly because that's the only thing we know. There are too many good people who die in accidents and from disease, while other less deserving people live prosperously, to think that a kind and benevolent God was controlling everyone's life."

"God works is mysterious ways—we can't hope to understand why he does what he does."

"You just have to have faith, huh.  That's a cop out and you know it."

 "Your reflections on the Four Ws of life have produced a rather skewed philosophy, Sam.  It may be that mine is more of a group philosophy than a personal one, and perhaps it slowly has changed over time.  I just don't remember thinking specifically about the four W's of life, or a philosophy of life, for that matter.  I go to church because everyone else goes, it serves humanitarian purposes, but I listen to my family for moral guidance."

"Yes, I know.  That's why I was so nervous about this evening.  What if your family hadn't approved of me? Would that change your feelings for me?"

"That's silly Sam; everyone loved you."

"Yes, I felt that, but what if that acceptance hadn't been there?  Would you continue to love me anyway?  What if you found out something about me that the family didn't like and they wanted you to leave me?  What if, even if you tried, you couldn't change their minds?  Would you stay with them or would you come with me?"

Charles looked at Sam with a frown.  "That's a meaningless question, Sam.  The family was taken with you and that's all there is to it."

"But does the family's opinion always determine your actions?" Sam persisted.

Still confused, Charles continued, "Certainly it's important to me that my family and I agree, but I don't see any conflict."

A waiter approached them and announced, "We'll be closing in five minutes Mr. Bennington, Ms. Mathews. We hope you had a good time and that we will see you again soon."

As Sam and Charles began to stroll toward the exit, Charles turned to Sam; "One of these days I'd like to hear your specific answers to the Four Ws."

"Ok, and maybe someday you can answer my questions about your family."

"Jeez, Sam I thought I did."

Sam laughed and said, "I have to use the ladies' room before we leave; excuse me?"  As she entered the ladies room she continued, "I'll meet you out front in a couple of minutes."

After she completed her touchup and exited the ladies' room, Sam entered the hallway leading to the lobby.  A man, whom she vaguely remembered as frequenting the club, intercepted her.  He put one hand on each of her shoulders saying, "Hi Sam, how the fuck are you?" Those words reminded her of the last time she had seen him. He was portly, homely, spoke incessantly in profanities as he continuously groped women.  Several women had pushed him away and admonished him to no avail.

The language and the man were repulsive to Sam and she responded in an irritated voice, "I'm ok Mr. Tubbs, but to you my name is Ms. Mathews."  She abruptly stepped back, hoping that he would recognize her displeasure.  Most normal males would have recognized the rebuff and retreated, but not Mr. Tubbs.  He reached around Sam's back and let his hand slide down and rest for a moment on her buttocks.

"How nice Mr. Tubbs.  May I have your hand for a second?"  Mr. Tubbs, with a broad self-satisfied smile, placed his meaty hand in Sam's.  As she stared into his eyes, a wild, savage look washed over her face releasing some of the emotions she had controlled for most of the evening following the pool house fiasco. All of her energy was focused on her grip and she began squeezing his hand progressively harder.  Her intent was to pulverize the meaty paw she held in her hand.  For a moment Mr. Tubbs was quite pleased with himself, then as reality replaced stupidity, the color in his face became as bright as the pain he felt in his hand.  His knees buckled and he began wilting to the floor.  Almost on his knees, he blurted out, "Please, Ms. Mathews, I didn't mean no fucking harm.  For gods sake, you're gonna break my fucking hand."

She made no reply; her concentration was totally focused on her mission.  It took a few seconds before she sensed another presence and hand on hers.  She instinctively applied even more pressure with her right hand.  Mr. Tubbs groaned in agony as she grabbed the intruding hand with her left hand and placed her left foot strategically behind the legs of the second person, and sent him sprawling to the floor.  She then released her grip on Mr. Tubbs, and with the wild fury of an angry savage, she flung her whole weight on a knee to the second assailants chest as she prepared to deliver a mortal, straight fingered thrust to his throat.

As she focused on her target, she saw a pair of soft blue eyes and a familiar face. "Sam, for gods sake, it's me." Charles was screaming. "Sam please, control yourself. Don't hit me!" He was shielding his face with his arms as if protecting himself from a wild Lion about to rip his face off.

Finally recognizing the second assailant as Charles, Sam rose and turned her anger back to Mr. Tubbs. As he worked his way to a standing position, Sam thrust her forearm to his throat and smashed him against the wall; his toes barely touched the floor. She then yelled, "The next time you touch me, I swear I'll cut off your balls, fry them in butter, and force them down your throat with a red hot poker. Do you understand?"

Mr. Tubbs was unable to speak because Sam's forearm was crushing his voice box. He blinked his bloodshot eyes and tried to nod his head affirmatively as best he could. Sam maintained her forearm position momentarily while she stared her victim in the eye, making sure he understood the magnitude of his inappropriate behavior. She then removed her arm and stepped away. He again slumped to the floor.

Charles was now sitting on the floor with his mouth wide open, having witnessed Sam's fury with complete astonishment. It was several minutes before he was able to speak. "Sam, please try to calm down. Everything is ok, nobody's trying to hurt you." He made no attempt to stand up for fear the movement would motivate Sam to knock him down again. He could still see the rage and anger in her eyes and he knew it would take more time before it was safe to approach her.

No one moved for several minutes as Sam basked in the exhilaration of expressing her rage in defense of a righteous cause. She soon recognized the need to control that rage and re-engage in civilized conduct again. But it takes time to shift to passive polite behavior as opposed to the almost instantaneous expression of uncontrolled rage. After her transition from angry savage to her normal self she said, matter of factly, "I'm sorry Charles. Some times the savage in me takes over, but I think she is back in her cage for now."

Charles still didn't move until Sam extended him her hand to help him up. "Sam, you scared the hell out of me. Where did all that anger come from?"

"I don't really know. I think it's always there, but sometimes I control it better than other times. This has been a particularly troublesome day. Are you ready to go?"

# *Chapter Eight*

In the car, after leaving the club, they headed toward Sam's house where CB had an open invitation to spend the night. Charles was the first to break a long silence, "You know Sam, during dinner you were witty, accepting of other people's opinions, conversed knowledgeably on every subject that came up, and everyone adored you. You made me very proud and happy that we are together."

"Thank you, sweetheart. Why do I feel there is a 'but' coming."

"Because there is. It concerns the incident it the hallway. There was intense, uncontrolled rage in your eyes and you became like a primordial savage fighting for food or something. I don't think I have that kind of monster in me."

"Well, maybe you're a better person than I am, or maybe you show your anger in more socially acceptable ways."

"You scared the hell out of me. I thought you were going to rip out my throat."

"You were right to be afraid; you were very close to getting seriously hurt. But I was just protecting myself. I thought someone else was attacking me. I didn't know it was you at first. You weren't supposed to be there."

"I was there because some lady came running down the hall and yelled that you were in trouble."

"So you were there to protect me?"

"Yes I was, but then you attacked me."

She paused briefly and then with her hand gently patting his cheek she playfully taunted, "Are you still afraid, you big baby?"

"Now that's not funny, I really thought you were going to kill me, and all I was trying to do was help you."

"I wonder what Mr. Tubbs thought?"

"You really hurt him.  I hope he doesn't sue you."

"But if he does, me hero will come to my rescue again, won't you?"

"I don't know.  You'll have to promise not to become that wild animal again."

"I'm sorry," Sam consoled. "He made me so angry that I didn't stop to think where I was or what I was doing."

Charles reached over and kissed her on the cheek and said, "Here's hoping there won't be a next time."

They sat in silence for some time and then Sam said, "There is something that still bothers me."

"And, what's that?"

"When you said that you and your family together decide what is important in your life, I can't help feeling that it would be the family rather than you that would make the decision with whom you spend your time and your life. That kind of scares me."

"But we talked about that. There's no problem because they thought you were great."

"Yes, you keep saying that, but what if there was a difference of opinion?"

"But that's not the case, so I just don't see the problem."

"Ok, ok I can see that this discussion is going nowhere. Just like our discussion about religion." She smiled, and then, "We'll just have to see how things play out. Maybe I'm just a worry wart."

While there was an obvious disconnect between their views regarding family and religion, they exchanged tender looks and gently squeezed each other's hand during a comfortable silence enjoyed by people in love. When they arrived at Sam's house, she punched in the security code at the gate and drove up the driveway.

As she reached to activate the garage door opener there was a loud bang and the driver's window shattered, throwing glass shards all over the front of the car. She felt a searing pain across her forehead as she screamed "CB, get out!"

She flung her door open and fell to the ground, simultaneously grasping the Glock nine-millimeter pistol she always carried strapped to her inner thigh. On the ground she kept rolling, attempting to determine the location of the shot while presenting a moving target herself. Finally she saw a flash as another shot rang out.

She returned fire in that general direction. There was a gasp followed by a thud, and breaking shrub branches.

Sam lay prone on the ground scanning the darkness for several moments. After what seemed an eternity with no return shots, she slowly rose to one knee; her gun still aimed in the general direction of the shots.

In a crouched position, gun in hand, she approached carefully the area from which the gunshots had come. As Sam visually searched the area, blood trickled into her eyes and she raised her hand to clear her vision. At that moment CB called out. "Sam… are you alright?"

After she was sure that the attacker was no longer a threat, she said, "Yeah, I'm alright; how about you?" More blood dripped into her eyes, and she wiped it away.

Charles came around the car to where Sam was standing. "My god what happened? All I heard was a lot of shooting; glass came splattering all over the place, you yelled at me. I jumped out of the car and hugged the ground, then everything was quiet. Sam you've got blood all over your face." Charles ranted aimlessly as he reached out to her.

"I'm not sure whether the shooter got a little bit of me or if I did it to myself. At any rate, everything seems to be working ok at the moment."

He saw the gun in her hand and said, "When I first noticed you carried a gun I was concerned and not very happy about it, but now I've changed my mind. Are you sure you're alright?"

"Yeah, I'm ok.  My heart is still on a joy ride though. Two wild incidents in one evening is a little much, even for me."

He took her into his arms and said, "What do you think the shooting was all about?"

Before she had a chance to answer, sirens of several approaching police cars broke the calm.

"How did they know that something was going on here?"  Sam asked.

"When all hell broke loose, I called 911 on my cell. That was the only thing I could think of doing."  The perspective of someone who has always been wealthy and sheltered from violence enabled him to deal well with the aftermath of violence but provided little to deal with defending against it.

Several police cars screeched to a stop with their headlights and spotlights flooding the scene.  Police officers jumped from their cars shouting, "Drop the weapon lady!  Drop it now and move away from each other!"

Both Charles and Sam were stunned by the demands, but Sam responded by dropping her gun and kicking it away from her.  "This is my home.  Somebody took several shots at us.  I had a gun and I defended myself. The gun is permitted."

She barely finished her matter of fact statements when several officers approached the couple and roughly drew their hands behind their backs.

"My purse is in the back seat," Sam continued in her deliberate tone. "There is plenty of identification to confirm what I'm saying."

"Ms. Mathews? Charles?" It was the voice of the Chief of Police as he approached the pair. "Take those cuffs off them. She lives here; I know these people."

The police officers did as they were told and the Chief continued, "What happened here, Ms. Mathews?"

"Just as I opened the garage door somebody took a shot at me from over there. Then I returned fire, but I never really saw what I was shooting at. That's about all I can tell you, Chief."

"Any idea who or why?"

"Not the foggiest. I'm pretty confused right now myself. I have the same questions that you have, but no answers. What I really need is some time to think and to clean up a little bit."

"Alright guys, search the area over there and tape off the scene," the chief said to his men. He then turned back to Sam and asked, "Where did you get the gun Sam?"

"I always carry a gun. I have all the permits."

"That's true Chief, she carries the gun all the time. When I questioned her about it, she showed me the permits."

Chief Watson scowled and replied, "That seems very odd to me, but we can check up on that later."

"Look Chief, we have told you everything we know. Neither one of us knows who the bad guy is or why he would be firing at us. Sam is wounded as you can obviously see."

"Let's go inside, maybe you can remember a few more details that will help the investigation," Chief Watson suggested. "Also, we can get a better look at that wound on your forehead."

"Chief, I don't mean to be belligerent or anything but I would like very much to just take Sam inside and get her a stiff drink. She can take a nice warm bath and try to get some sleep. Then maybe she can better answer your questions. There is plenty of time for the inquisition tomorrow."

After some hesitation, and being well aware of the prestige of the couple, Chief Watson said, "Well you're lucky that I was riding along with the patrol tonight. Otherwise they would have you on your way downtown right now. We'll continue our investigation out here tonight, and then I want to talk to you both first thing in the morning. Things like this just don't happen around here and we've got to get to the bottom of it. Go ahead; take her inside, Charles. I'll see you in the morning."

"Thank you Chief, I do appreciate this. I'll tell you everything I know in the morning, but unfortunately it probably won't be much," responded Sam as she and Charles went into the house.

Once inside, Sam turned to Charles, "CB, will you be a dear and grab a bottle of wine and a couple of glasses?

I'll go up and draw us a bath, I feel like a soiled rag."

"Sure, that's a great idea, that should calm us down a bit."

CB selected a mellow Pinot Noir and grabbed two large bowled glasses from the cupboard, then made his way upstairs. As he entered the bedroom, Sam was at the window overlooking the pool area. She was very concerned that the police would find Ramon's body in the pool and demand an explanation. She had to be prepared not only for questions about the shooting but also about Ramon and she was not prepared for either.

When she heard CB, she began undressing for her bath and threw her clothes in a pile ready for the cleaners. She took her time, aware that he was watching from the doorway.

She then slowly made her way to the bathroom to take a look at her still bloody forehead. After examining her wound in the mirror she opened the medicine cabinet and retrieved the peroxide and cotton balls for the necessary repair work.

Charles marveled at her soft yet well-defined muscularity and fluid, graceful movements. He entered a pleasant dream world and was struck by how succeeding moments in time can radically change emotions. Earlier in the evening he feared that Sam was going to rip his throat out, just a few moments ago he was terrified that he was going to be shot dead, and now the naked body of the woman he loved was pleasantly arousing him. Go figure.

CB followed Sam into the bathroom, wine bottle and glasses in hand, but other things on his mind. He placed the bottle and glasses on a small stool next to the bathtub and then took a cotton ball, soaked in peroxide, and gently stroked Sam's forehead.

"Good lord Sam, that was close; it's a miracle that you weren't killed. What a horrible experience; I damn near died of fear, and there you were, wounded and fighting like a Green Beret—again."

"Ouch! Damn! I may act like a Beret but I still feel pain."

"Sorry sweetheart; I guess for a moment there I thought you were superhuman." He kissed her forehead gently and then, examining her wound said, "You know, this is as much a burn as a cut. I think you just might live."

"Very funny," she scolded and then added, "You spend more time staring at my boobs than you do my wound."

"I do not."

"Yes you do."

"You must admit they are beautiful."

"They are just milk emitting biological appliances," she scolded. "I have never understood why men are so fascinated with them."

"I have a theory."

"So you have a boob fascination theory. Ok, smarty pants, enlighten me."

"Well when you're first thrust into this strange world from your mother's womb, somebody roughly grabs and rubs you all over with an abrasive towel. Then maybe someone else smacks you on the butt until you cry, and does a bunch of other disagreeable things. It's very frightening. But then they throw you naked on your mother's belly and your head rests between these two soft, warm, cuddly bubbles. Your mother makes goo-goo noises and holds you gently in her arms and makes everything seem ok again."

"That's it. That's your boob theory?"

"No, there is more to it."

"It better be good."

"After this first pleasant experience with boobs, somebody grabs you away and does all sorts of other unpleasant things to you. Just when you think you've been thrust into hell, they bring you back to mom. She holds you gently and rubs your mouth with the nipple of one of her breasts. Finally a small drip of milk splashes on your lips and when you lick it off you find it to have a very pleasant flavor. So you open your mouth and in plunges' the nipple. You begin to suck; you like it a lot, and the boob fetish is born. There," he said with great satisfaction.

"So when men gape at women's breasts they think about suckling their mother's breast?" Sam said with disbelief.

"No dummy, they think of something very pleasant

and comforting in an otherwise hostile world."

"That's the dumbest thing I have ever heard."

"That's my theory, and I'm sticking with it."

"What about girls, they have the same experience, and they don't worship boobs."

"Oh but they do in their own way, but you'll have to come up with your own explanation of that. I can't do all the creative thinking here."

"Alright, that's enough about boobs, funny man. Let's get into the tub; this fighting machine is looking for some action."

They quickly removed his clothing and entered the tub, playfully splashing and massaging every body part that could be reached. After the playfulness they poured a glass of wine and reheated the water. Sam sat between Charles' legs with her back to him and her head on his shoulder with his arms around her. They sat this way for several minutes silently sipping and savoring their wine and resting.

Eventually Charles blurted out "Sam why would someone want to hurt you? People don't go around shooting at someone for no reason."

"I know; I can't figure it out. But what may be a good reason to the shooter may not be to me. I was thinking about who it might have been and why and there is only one thing that comes to mind."

"What's that?"

"Unknowingly, maybe I did something to someone that they didn't like. You read things in the paper all the time. Maybe it was a mistake; maybe they thought I was someone else. Hell, maybe they were after you. Did you ever think of that?"

"No way. Are you kidding me? Nobody would want to shoot at me. I'm the nicest guy in town."

"Oh, so you think I'm not a nice guy?"

"You know what I mean. It's just so strange; just doesn't make sense. Who the hell would have something against you?"

"Well things don't always happen for a good reason. Maybe we'll never be able to figure it out."

"But we have to or maybe it will happen again."

"That is a scary thought." She pondered for a moment and then said, "I don't mean to change the subject entirely, but I was wondering; when someone does something bad, like shooting at someone, do they change in some way or are they simply perceived differently?"

"How did we get to that subject? We were talking about somebody shooting at us and all of a sudden you're asking about people's perceptions. Do we have to get philosophical again?"

"Yeah. It's a good question." She exclaimed.

"I don't know! Sometimes you bewilder me."

"Come on sweetie. What do you think? If a person

does something bad, does it change that person in some way, or are they just perceived differently by others and themselves?"

"Well, sometimes perception is reality I guess. I mean if people knew that someone had done something bad in the past, they probably would perceive that person with some skepticism and treat them differently, at lease initially."

"So you think it's just perception?"

"Let me finish. By the same token doing something bad may change the chances that that person would do something bad again—depending upon whether or not they were repentant. I can see where doing something bad could change a person for the better, if that person was determined to never do it again."

"So you think it can actually change a person?"

"I think it can do both. But in general I think people think badly of people who do bad things, unless there was a morally compelling reason for doing what they did. Now can we drop it?"

"I'm impressed. Now, if I told you that I had done something bad in the past, would that change your feelings for me now?"

"Sweetheart there isn't anything, I mean anything, in this world that would change the way I feel about you. If you did something bad, I know you must have had a good reason for it."

"Then you're saying that the ends justify the means?"

"Well…. Now you're just being argumentative."

"No, not really.  I'm just asking if the person that shot at me had a good reason, should he be perceived as a bad person or not?"

"Sweetheart I can tell that these questions are important to you and you seem to be bothered about being perceived as good or bad."

"Well isn't everyone."

"I can tell you without reservation that no matter what bad things you have done in the past; it will not affect the way I feel about you now."

"Oh that's so sweet, and the same goes for me."

"But I must say I'm beginning to feel like a prune in this tub.  Can we towel off and get into bed?  It's very late and we have to be up early to meet with the Chief."

"OK.  I'm beginning to feel a bit pickled myself."

As she was drying off she made her way to the window overlooking the pool to see what the police were doing. She prayed that they would not find Ramon's body and roust her out of bed in the middle of the night.

After drying off she slipped under the covers and wrapped her naked body around Charles' and they both tried to get some sleep using the comfort and warmth of each other as a sedative.

She slept restlessly throughout the night, searching her

dreams for an acceptable explanation for Ramon lying dead at the bottom of her pool.

# *Chapter Nine*

Someone banging on the back door and ringing the doorbell startled CB and Sam awake in the morning. She donned her robe and slippers, went downstairs, opened the back door and was confronted by a police officer.

"Ma'am, Chief Watson wants you to come to the pool area. There is something there he wants you to see."

Sam knew what was there and took time to respond. There was just one answer she could give, but it took her several seconds to get it out. "Tell him I'll be right there. I've got to put on some clothes."

"Yes ma'am, but make it snappy. The Chief is pretty upset."

"Ok, ok. I said I'd be right there!"

Sam hurried upstairs and pulled on a pair of jeans and a man's shirt, combed her hair and refreshed her face, all the while shaping her alibi for the preceding afternoon. "I don't know when he died so how could I know if I was home. I never saw anything. I am very upset that something like this could happen in my pool. I would be willing to pay for the funeral because he was hurt on my property."

CB stirred sleepily in bed and looked at his watch, "Who the hell is it at seven o'clock in the morning."

"It's Chief Watson. He's continuing his investigation

of last night."

"Oh, good lord. I almost forgot. Tell him I'll be right down." He struggled out of bed and began to dress.

Sam was headed downstairs and didn't acknowledge him. Upon reaching the kitchen door she was still silently rehearsing her story. Crossing the patio, she could see a couple of people seated and standing around one of the tables near the pool. The Chief was there along with another man in a suit, who she thought must be a detective. Seated with his back to Sam, there was a man wearing a turban of some kind. She could also see two uniformed officers, one in the pool house and the other looking around the yard.

As she approached, the Chief Watson rose and said, "Good morning Ms. Mathews, I hope you were able to get some sleep last night. How is your wound?"

"I slept well. The wound is just minor, thank you Chief."

"That's good. We were around here until after one a.m. When we got back about a half-hour ago we found this guy carrying some things from the pool area and putting them into his truck. He says he knows you."

As Sam reached the table, the man with the turban turned and said in a weak voice, "I get my things."

Sam stared at the man. It wasn't a turban on his head; it was bandages. She could barely make out his face. "Oh, my God", she blurted out. She felt pain in her throat and stomach; she became flushed and couldn't speak. All of the rehearsing she had done was useless. Finally with an unnatural voice, she exclaimed, "Ramon?"

"Si." His blackened eyes peered from the bandages. Muted, they stared at each other, for several minutes not knowing how to proceed.

Sam was thinking, "How can this be? I couldn't feel a pulse. I threw him in the pool. Doesn't he remember what happened? What has he told the Chief? Now what do I do?"

Finally after what must have seemed an eternity, Chief Watson said. "I take it you know each other?"

After more silence, Sam gathered herself to very quietly say, "Ramon cleans the pool."

Ramon explained, "I here to clean pool yesterday. I fell, hit head then into pool. Hanged to pool long time. Got to steps and lay on deck long time. Dark when I call wife on cell. Went to hospital. I come here now to get things."

"So you say you were in the hospital all night?"

"Si."

"Did you see or hear anything yesterday afternoon, Ms. Mathews?" one of the detectives inquired.

"I didn't see anything. I might have been at the club, I don't know. What time did it happen."

Still in shock she spoke in short spurts; one thought running into another. She knew she sounded stupid but was unable to elevate her conversation from the moronic level.

"Can I go?  I don't feel so good," Ramon said as he shakily rose from his chair.

"Yes, you may go," responded Chief Watson.  "But don't leave town; we may need to talk to you further." As Ramon wobbled toward his truck, Chief Watson asked, "By the way what kind of gun do you own Ramon?"

Ramon stopped and was silent for a few seconds.  He turned and looked at Sam.  After a few more seconds of silence, he said, "I don't got no gun."

"Oh, really.  And what brand of cigarette do you smoke?"

"I no smoke."  After glaring at Sam for a few more seconds he turned to leave, and a police officer escorted him to his truck.

"That's a strange dude, Sam. How long has he been with you?"

"I can't remember exactly Chief; a year maybe." Sam was wondering why Ramon hadn't told the truth. "What was his game?  Might he have done the shooting?" She was very puzzled and deep in thought. As time elapsed, she became more comfortable and in command of her faculties.

"I described what happened last night to Inspector Casey," Charles said as he approached the Chief and Sam. "He said I should talk to you before leaving, Chief.

I really do have to get to work."

"Ok, you can go. Casey is pretty thorough. I'll get the information I need from him to compare with what Ms. Mathews has to say."

"Thanks, good luck with the investigation."

"Give me a call later, Charles," Sam called after him. "I think I'm close to making that deal on the Chandler Building and I need to hear what you think."

"Ok, Sam. I'll call you this afternoon. Good luck." Charles hurried away and made no attempt to hold or kiss her goodbye.

Sam turned toward Chief Watson as he asked, "Ok Sam. Tell me what the hell went down here last night."

Sam related the story from the time she left for the party until she arrived back at the house. She tried to recall every detail.

"So you were not at home when Ramon says he fell into the pool?"

"Well like I said, I didn't see anything out of the ordinary. I didn't know he was here and I don't know when he fell. How would he know if I was home or not? Maybe I was, maybe I wasn't."

"Yeah I guess so; he parked his truck behind the hedge so it's pretty hard to see from the house. Tell me again why you carry a gun."

"Well I know it's a little unusual Chief, but I just

feel safer when I do. I've got all the permits and have had them for years. I go to the range weekly and I'm comfortable with many types of guns."

The Chief, ignoring Sam's' last statement, continued. "But strapped to your thigh. What's that all about?"

"God damn it Chief, that's what I like to do. It's not a crime is it?"

"No, I guess not—not if you have all the right permits," the Chief said as if he had been punched. "In this case it was probably a good thing that you had a gun and the wit to use it. That's unusual for a professional woman living in this neighborhood, don't you think?"

"Look Chief, I'll grant you that women don't ordinarily carry guns and know how to use them. But the fact that someone actually tried to shoot me must make my rationale for carrying a gun make sense to you."

"Well it makes sense if you were expecting trouble. Do you feel that your life is in danger?"

"No, not really. I just feel more comfortable when I'm prepared for whatever may happen."

"You don't strike me as someone who is so insecure that you need to carry a gun all the time. I'm sure there is an underlying cause there Sam, but for whatever reason, you don't feel you can tell me about it."

"I'm not all that insecure. Some women carry mace. I carry a gun because I know how to use it and it's a more reliable method of defense."

"We'll let it pass for now, but I think we may have to revisit it depending how the investigation goes."

"Thanks very much," Sam said sarcastically.

"Anyway, we found four spent 45mm cartridges over there in the bushes where you said the shots came from. There were also a few drops of blood we're having analyzed."

"That sounds encouraging."

"The shooter had apparently been waiting for some time, there were three cigarette butts on the ground. You know any smokers who may have a reason to take a shot at you?"

"Chief I don't know anyone who had a reason for shooting at me, period."

"We also found five cartridges from your gun. Why did you take so many shots? Did you see anyone?"

"I only saw the gun flash so I really didn't have anything to aim at. As you might suspect, I was trying to hit the son-of-a-bitch, or at least scare him off. Apparently I hit him, but not where it made him bleed a lot. Too bad; I wish you had found his dead body."

"That's cold Sam. Damn cold." A little stunned the Chief paused, then "I think that's about it for the time being." As he rose to leave he said, "Call me if you think of anything else, ok?"

"Sure, Chief. If I have a revelation I'll let you know. And thanks for handling this personally. I know you've got a lot on your plate."

The chief and his entourage gathered their equipment and started to leave.  To a man, they thought a little bit differently about Sam than they had before this incident. She wasn't a typical victim; they felt that the assailant was the underdog in last night's confrontation.

# *Chapter Ten*

Sam and Charles lay in bed unable to fall asleep the night after the shooting. "Sam you were very quiet during dinner and the drive home tonight," Charles observed as he caressed her forehead with his hand. "You seem preoccupied about something. Last night's fireworks still bothering you?"

Since the shooting, Sam had been confused about how much she should tell Charles about her past, because she was developing a fondness for him and the Bennington family. Unless it became absolutely necessary, she didn't want to confess the true nature of Josh's business for obvious reasons. If however, as she surmised, the shooting had been directed at her because someone had become aware of her background, or that Mr. Wolf had found her, Charles needed to be warned. She hesitated, because such a disclosure could destroy their relationship and maybe send her to jail. However she already felt responsible for the death of Charles' sister—even though she had known nothing about it and had not pulled the trigger. She just could not bear it if she also became indirectly responsible for Charles' death.

Sam lay quietly evaluating all the facts before responding. "I need to tell you something about my past, but I haven't done so until now because I'm afraid of the consequences. I've been struggling with this dilemma for some time, but the shooting has forced my hand and now I have no choice. It's the kind of thing that will put a burden on both of us." Sam paused to look into Charles eyes as if trying to divine his reaction to her real background; still uncertain she cautiously continued, "You must swear that you will not tell another soul what I am about to tell you. Not even your family—especially not your family. Do I have your word?"

"That sounds ominous Sam, what the hell are you talking about?"

"Do you swear?"

"Yes, of course. If you don't want me to repeat what you say, then I won't. You can trust me."

Sam sighed, "I have to start with a little history."

"That's ok, I want to know everything about you."

"Shortly after I started college I met Josh who was several years older. He was coming back to school after working in his family's business for several years. We were mutually attracted and soon we began to spend a lot of time together. He loved guns and took me to the shooting range regularly and taught me to be a crack shot. Guns of all types were scattered around his apartment."

"Guns, why guns for heavens sake?"

"Guns were a hobby for him. We took trips into the countryside to run and sometimes shoot. He wanted me to be in top physical shape and a crack shot; he took pride in that. He would push me until I was exhausted."

"That doesn't sound like much fun," Charles sneered.

"On one occasion we went to one of those war game simulations in the wilderness. It was serious training, almost as if we were training to become Green Berets. The weekend after that, we decided to take some down time, and flew to Las Vegas. We were so infatuated that on impulse we decided to get married while we were there. Thinking back, it's almost surreal. I didn't think about the practical aspects of marriage, just that now I would be with Josh forever."

"After returning from Las Vegas we continued our training routine. He and I ran marathons two or three times a year, worked out regularly at the gym and practiced hand-to-hand-combat. Being pushed beyond the limits of my endurance trying to keep up made me stronger than I ever thought I could be. At the same time, always being second best made me feel inferior to him and my feeling of self worth became very dependent upon his approval. That was the first time in my life that I felt dependent on someone other than myself."

"Good lord Sam, he sounds like a nut or a neo Nazi. Didn't you get a little concerned about him, even scared?"

"Not really. I had never been so in awe of anybody in my life. Not even the father I loved above all. Josh took trips by himself occasionally, but never asked me to go with him. When he was gone I felt anxious. Sometimes when he was gone, I felt aimless, didn't know what to do with myself. I asked him about the trips and he just said that it was better that I didn't know anything about them; they just helped pay the bills. But the trips made me progressively more anxious. He would be gone anywhere from a couple days to a week, and when he came back, he wouldn't tell me anything about where he'd been or what he'd done."

"What was he trying to hide?"

"Well I pestered him so badly that he finally said that I could come with him on a trip, but that I would have to stay in the hotel room by myself for some time. Glad to be invited along, I said that would be OK as long as we got to spend more time together."

"So what did he do on his trips?"

"Hold on, I'm getting to it. The first trip went ok. I stayed in the room, and he was gone about four hours. When he returned he wouldn't tell me where he'd been. About two weeks later he said he had to go on another trip, and this time I could help him if I wanted. So of course I was all excited and said that I would be very happy to help him. I still didn't know what he was doing, but any chance of helping him, whatever it was, felt good. When we got there, he explained that all I had to do was get dressed provocatively and go to the desk of a certain hotel and ask the desk clerk if a certain person was registered. If so, I was to say that I was Shirley and I would be waiting for him in a car parked at the curb. Then I was to go back to our hotel room and wait for Josh. After everything was settled, we got ready and left our hotel together. He took the briefcase that held one of his high powered rifles. When I asked why he had the case, he said he needed to show the rifle to a dealer who was thinking of buying it from him. I did what he asked and he came back to the hotel about an hour later, said thank you, and took me out to dinner."

"This is getting more and more strange. Did you finally find out what Josh was up to?"

"Well the strangest part was that when we were getting ready for bed that night, I heard on the TV that the same guy I had asked about that afternoon had been shot to death in front of his hotel. It was all over the news. First of all Josh said he didn't want to talk about it, but I just would not leave it alone. Finally in the wee hours of the morning he admitted he shot the guy and that he, Josh, was in the murder-for-hire business."

"Oh my God, you can't be serious. You're making this up, right?"

"I wish it were a fairy tale. You can imagine how shocked I was. I told him I didn't want to see him again. I packed up, left the hotel room, and headed back to school. I moved in temporarily with a friend who had a spare room. But we saw each other almost every day at school, and he would not let go. He told me I was his wife and nothing I could do would change that. He vowed he would never give me a divorce. Throughout all this, no matter how much I told myself that I could never go back with him, his hold over me was just too great for me to overcome. He ended up telling me how he was raised in the family business and that they would only take contracts on really bad criminals and therefore they were doing a public service. He also went into the financial end of it, including that we owed our livelihood to the "business," and how much he was making—about the numbered Swiss bank accounts—everything. I was repulsed by what he told me but I was young, impressionable, completely naïve, and I felt that I could change him in time. I know none of these things added up to a good excuse, but finally I agreed to get back together with him, and sadly I eventually got involved with the family business."

Charles was horrified, "You mean to tell me you became an assassin?"

"No, I've never killed anyone!" Sam cried out. "I became his partner. He invested in several legitimate businesses to help launder the money and he set things up so that if anything happened to him I would be well taken care of financially."

"Holy smokes Sam, this is really hard to believe. Is that the source of all your money?"

"I told you that you would be shocked and that you might look at me differently knowing these things. Sadly, I haven't even told you the worst part yet."

"I'm not sure I want to hear any more."

"There is a lot more but, I'll make it brief. Shortly after we graduated from college, Josh and I went to Cancun to meet someone about new business. It turned out the whole trip had been a setup, and he was specifically targeted by some unknown organization or past client, and Josh was murdered. His killers threw his body in a trash barrel, filled it with gasoline, and set it on fire. I witnessed the whole thing; it was the most horrible thing I have ever seen in my life. I was paralyzed with grief, so stunned I couldn't breathe, and I passed out." Tears drenched her eyes as she clutched Charles and sobbed uncontrollably.

Charles waited for several minutes as he tried to digest the details he had just heard. "That must have been excruciating for you at the time and I'm sure the retelling is not any easier. Are you sure you want to go on with this?"

After several minutes of soft weeping Sam continued, "I have to tell you everything CB, you must know so that you can better protect yourself."

Silent tears kept sliding down her cheeks for some time, and then she continued, "After Josh was killed, my whole world went into a tailspin and I went home to live with my parents, as I've told you. The situation was particularly devastating to me because, in addition to losing Josh I had to deal with the realization that he— and by association, I—had been doing this same type of thing to other people for years. We killed people for money, without regard to the pain for the victims and their families. That awareness just never was factored into my thinking until I lost Josh in that terrible way. The guilt for our past actions, added to the grief of losing Josh, was more than I could deal with and I vowed to never again be involved with Josh's family or their business. I had long talks with my parents about good and evil, hope and redemption, God and the universe; anything that helped move me closer to accepting myself as a worthwhile person, even though I had done so many terrible things. I'm not sure that I could have gotten myself back together without my folks."

Charles wiped away the tears that gushed from Sam's eyes and down her face. "You were very lucky to have parents as nurturing as they were. I'm not sure that many parents would have had the strength or understanding, and most importantly the forgiveness."

"Dad was in turn disgusted, horrified, and incredibly angry. In time he relented a little and acknowledged that it was my problem to work out. It took a long time, but just as I was getting to understand my emotions and how to deal with them, my parents were both killed in an auto accident. When I first got the call telling me of the accident, I was terrified, then fell into a vacuum of despair. I just felt there wasn't anything left to live for. That gloom and fear drove me out of my parent's home. I didn't purposefully plan to come to Crown City. It just was on my way, somewhat familiar, and I felt that its beauty and comfort could give me a new beginning—and safety."

Charles waited a short time while he contemplated the significance of this new information, and then, "I'm sorry for your loss, Sam. Family can be the center of a person's universe and when they are all gone, there isn't much left. It leaves a vacuum—the ultimate aloneness."

"Yes that's just the way I felt. It was very painful."

"It took enormous strength to raise yourself from that depth, you should be proud of that. At the same time,

I'm having a really hard time digesting all the rest."

Sam extended her hand, and Charles reached and took it into his own. They held onto each other as they gathered their thoughts and then Charles asked, "So Josh was killed not too long before you came here, is that right?"

"Yes."

"Then he was killed a couple of weeks after Mr. Chandler and Carolyn were killed?"

"Yes, that sounds about right. You sound like what I said reminded you of Mr. Chandler and Carolyn?"

"I don't know. So many deaths, so close together... I just remember what you said at the folk's the other day. Somehow they got linked in my mind."

They sat quietly for some time as Sam cried and CB comforted her. He felt a great compassion for her tragic loses. At the same time he wrestled with the troubling information about Sam's background.

Finally Sam continued. "All this took place some time ago, but the reason I felt it was necessary to tell you this now is that I think someone from my past has tracked me down. They may be trying to kill me for the same reason that Josh was killed. If that's the case, you could be in danger just by being with me—like the other night. That's why I felt I had to tell you all this stuff. I must protect you even though it could damage our future together and get me into a lot of trouble if other people found out about it."

"I appreciate your concern Sam.  I'm not sure what to do about all this right now, I need some time to think."

The two of them stared at the ceiling with tear-drenched eyes.  One exhausted by the effort of unloading painful memories, and the other crushed by their weight and implications.

# *Chapter Eleven*

Charles entered his father's house in a very agitated state, and the two of them made their way to the study. "You seem a little unraveled Charles, you've been out of town for a while; I thought you would be refreshed when you returned. Let me pour you a little brandy to calm you down." He poured a couple of snifters, took one to Charles and then sat in his favorite chair. "Now what's bothering you?"

Taking the brandy Charles said solemnly, "Father I had a very disturbing discussion with Sam right before I went to New York. I should have told you before I left, but I needed time to think it through because Sam asked me not to tell anyone about it."

"Well what is it?"

"It seems that the person who we contracted to shoot Chandler and who we had shot for killing Carolyn, was Sam's husband at the time."

"What do you mean, Sam's husband?"

"Just what I said. Sam confessed to me that her husband was in a murder-for-hire business."

"What—you're crazy!"

"Not only that, she knew all about it. In fact, from time to time, she went on the trips with him."

"I can't believe that. That's not her."

"Don't get me wrong; she said she's never killed anyone, but she was in the know. She said her husband was killed a couple of weeks after you took the contract out on Mr. Chandler. It turns out that the man you hired was Sam's husband."

"She told you that?"

"She told me that shortly after her husband killed Mr. Chandler; he was killed in Cancun in exactly the same way that we were told our contract was fulfilled. That is just too big a coincidence not to be the same guy."

"Good lord Charles, that's staggering. I can't believe that Sam was once in the murder-for-hire business. How can you be sure?"

"For god's sake dad, she told me. She didn't want to, but given the shooting the other night at her house, she is convinced that someone is out to kill her like they did her husband. She's afraid that, if I'm with her I may get hurt. She confessed everything so that I could better protect myself. I'm still trying to come to grips with the whole thing. As awful as it sounds, I'm sure she's telling the truth; if not, what would she have to gain by telling me all that stuff?"

"So she loves you enough to expose herself in order to protect you?"

"That's what she said. Of course I didn't say anything to her about our involvement."

"Of course not; that would be suicide. She might have shot you right on the spot. Damn, I have trouble thinking of her in that way. She really took us in. Not a word to your mother; this has to be strictly between you and me. Is that understood?"

"That goes without saying. But the question is what we do with this information."

"That depends on why she came here I guess." Mr. Bennington rubbed his chin with his hand and continued, "I don't think it's because she wanted to start a new life and forget the past, or she would not have chosen Crown City."

"She said she just came here by chance," Charles said as he rose and strode around the room. "More likely she came here because she found out that we put the hit on her husband and she wants revenge. Being in the 'business' she would know where the contract came from."

"But does she know who was responsible for the orders," Mr. Bennington said as he joined his son parading about the room with drink in hand. "Maybe she is here to find out exactly who had her husband killed; that would make her very dangerous to both of us."

"Well, it could be any one of those possibilities," Charles agreed. "My guess is that she is here for revenge and I think we have to do something about it before she discovers the truth. I'm just not sure what that something should be, because I love her."

"Your feelings be damned, Charles. I'm not going to let that little snake come up and bite me in the ass. We've got to get rid of her."

"No, I can't do that. That is not an option."

"You wouldn't need to have anything to do with it. I'll take care of everything. The good thing is that, somebody's already taken a shot at her, and the police think they know who it is. If she were killed, nobody would think it came out of the blue. No big investigation would need to be undertaken. It would be perfect."

"I know dad, but we don't have absolute proof that she is here for revenge, nor are we sure that she would ever find out the truth. I couldn't do anything to hurt her before I knew for sure what her intentions are."

"You're a sentimental fool, Charles. We need to take action now, before it's too late. The alternative is too awful to contemplate."

"But I just can't have her killed unless it's absolutely necessary, and I won't let you do it until then. Just remember that we're already responsible for an innocent death. I won't ever get over our role in Carolyn's death."

"I think that's a mistake Charles—but for your sake I guess I could forgo action for the time being. Maybe you can keep seeing her for a while so we can keep an eye on her and try to find out for sure what she's up to."

"How can I possibly act as if nothing has changed? She would know there was something different in our relationship, and that might lead her to suspect us of something. I think the only thing I can do is to break it off with her and just let the chips fall where they may."

"I don't like leaving things to chance."

"If I don't see her for a while maybe I can get my emotions together. In the meantime we can still keep a close eye on her and see what she's up to."

"I don't know, I'm afraid that breaking up is going to cause her to look at us even more closely than if you stay with her."

"Maybe so dad, but I just can't be around her all the time and not give myself away. I know myself too well. It just won't work."

"I don't like it, but I see your point. You've always been too sentimental for your own good. I still think we should do something now, but I agree we don't want to take that step unless it's absolutely necessary. We're already too deep into this underworld stuff as it is. Do what you have to do, and I'll set up 24-hour surveillance on her."

At that point, Charles' cell phone rang. "I better take it. Hello, Charles here."

"Hi Charles, you're back! How did your trip go?"

Charles was startled to hear Sam's voice; he paused briefly and then, "Hello Sam. The trip went fine, but it is nice to be home again."

"When did you get back?"

"Oh a couple of days ago."

"And you didn't call me?"

"I didn't know just what to do.  Guess I needed some time to rest and think."

"Yes I guess I did give you a big load to carry."

"What you told me was certainly the major part—it has been very difficult to deal with."

"Do you feel like you're ready to talk about it over lunch?"

Charles gave his father a dismayed shrug and then continued with the telephone conversation.  "I guess so.  Things make a little more sense now that I've had a long chat with father, and time to think things through.  Lunch sounds fine."

"You didn't tell your dad what I told you, did you?"

"No, of course not.  We were just discussing business."

"That's good.  You had me worried there for a moment.  How about one o'clock; we can stretch it out a little if we need too.  We should discuss the Chandler Building deal as well.  Things are heating up."

"We definitely need to talk Sam; things are in a very confusing state.  Hey, got to go.  See you at one at the club. OK?"

Charles closed his cell and examined his father's face a few seconds, sighed, and then stated in a melancholy voice,  "I guess I have to go tell Sam that I can't see her any more. I don't know how I'm going to do it, but it's the only way. Wish me luck; I'll let you know how things turn out."

"Ok son, good luck. I know you will handle the situation as reasonably as you can. I'll get things started on my end."

***

As Charles waited at the Club he reflected on the details of Josh's death. The relationship between Josh's death and the Bennington family was absolutely necessary to keep secret. Charles and his father had arranged—through an underground contact—to kill Mr. Chandler, who was about to expose a shady political deal that Charles' father had made. If the information was made public, everything that the Bennington name and fortune stood for would have been destabilized, and four generations of hard work would have been wiped out. The elder Mr. Bennington would never let that happen. No amount of persuasion or money could stop Mr. Chandler. In a fit of panic, the senior Bennington made arrangements for the hit during which Carolyn was accidentally killed. In anger and grief, Mr. Bennington and Charles had then made arrangements for the elimination of the hit man responsible for Carolyn's death. The hit man had apparently been Josh, as the unique circumstances of his death, as related by Sam, revealed. This couldn't be coincidence. Sam must know that the contract came from Crown City. Had she found out that the Benningtons were the ones who had fingered her husband? Charles struggled to find a way to tell Sam that their relationship could not continue.

***

Meanwhile on the way to the club Sam turned over in her mind the events of the last few weeks. "I let my emotions get the better of me when I clubbed Ramon and I didn't do much better with the shooting. As I said to the Chief, I would have been more satisfied if the perpetrator was lying there dead. That was not a wise thing to say to the Chief of Police I guess. Perhaps in the long run, what I confessed to Charles might have a more profound effect on my life. How is he going to deal with those revelations? He seemed a little distant on the phone. I felt at the time that I had to tell him. If someone from my past is out to get me and CB and I are together, he could be in danger too. How could I not tell him no matter the consequences? But now, with Ramon still alive, he seems to be the more logical candidate, so I'm having second thoughts. What a mess. Did I do the right thing?"

Sam waved and joined Charles seated at a table in the dinning room. "Hi sweetheart. Sorry I'm a little late."

"That's all right Sam, I think I may have been a little early." She kissed him and sat down at the table just as the waiter arrived.

"What will it be folks? Or would you rather hear the specials of the day?"

"Oh I don't feel adventuresome today Toby, just bring me the usual. How about you Sam?"

"I'll start with a double martini straight up and then I'll

have the usual."

"Very good ma'am, I'll return shortly with your drink."

"It's been over a week since I've heard from you, Charles. What's going on?"

"I had a lot to think through, Sam. The events of the last few weeks have been weighing on me, I guess."

"Things like what?"

"Well you know, the shooting, the story you related, everything."

"Have you come to any conclusions?"

"Well the whole thing is very disturbing and difficult for me. First the shooting. God I'm still shaking. Then you with the gun, your husband's business, it's hard to explain how I feel, let alone face the rest of the family."

"Thank goodness you're not going to tell them anything. Some of them are very narrow minded."

"I'm also having trouble reconciling what you told me about your past with what you've seemed to be since I've known you. If somebody else had told me that story, I would have called them a liar."

"It was the most intense and overwhelming time of my life. Josh was a guru who stole my mind; sabotaged my moral compass. Sometimes when I reflect about my past with Josh, I find it hard to believe that I could have gone along with things. It really bothers me now when I think about it. So I have some idea about how you must be feeling."

"It sounds like you're still troubled by your past."

"You can say that again, but I have to acknowledge that part of my life and deal with it. I can't let that period of depravity define the rest of my life. I have accepted responsibility for it and vowed to make amends as best I can."

"Do you think you will ever be able to love anyone like that again?"

"I will never let someone take over my mind like that again. When I reflect on it, I don't think it was love. The naïve and impressionable girl that I was, I think I was completely overwhelmed and dazzled. No way would I like to experience that again."

"I wish you hadn't told me all that stuff."

"I only told you about it so that you could better protect yourself. Now I'm more concerned that it is chasing you away from me."

"I'm concerned too, Sam. That type of background and the implications it has for my family is hard for me to accept. I'm not dealing with it very well. My father was very upset as well."

"Oh Christ, you told your father? What about your promise not to tell anyone?"

"I just thought I needed some advice. There is more to it than I thought. I was stunned and I needed father's advice."

"Damn. If I thought I couldn't trust you I would never have told you. I was just trying to protect you."

They sat in silence trying to determine where the conversation should go next. Charles couldn't tell Sam about the relationship between Josh's death and his father, and he was at a loss for how to tell Sam that they had to split up.

Disturbed and feeling the need to change the subject, Sam finally broke the silence. "As I said earlier, the Chandler deal is heating up. I talked to Mrs. Chandler after I talked to you. Neither of her kids wants to run the business, so she is pretty anxious to sell the building and distribute the proceeds to them. Everyone gets their money and goes his own way. She is still grieving for Mr. Chandler and doesn't need the building to remind her of him all the time."

Absent-mindedly Charles responded, "Did you talk price?"

"Yes, she likes the fact that the building would stay in local hands. She'll take ten mil if you and I are the buyers."

"I know the building will require substantial refurbishing, but even so that's a good price."

"So what do you think, shall we do it?"

"I don't know Sam, I like the price, but with all this other stuff I'm not sure I can make the commitment right now. I'm just unsure about things. Do you think she will hold the deal for a while?"

"I can ask. You seemed so sure just a couple of weeks ago. Has what I told you changed your mind?"

"Yes; I told you I was having trouble dealing with your background, the shooting and everything. It's going to be hard to reconcile all that with the family."

"So now you're concerned that your family won't accept me if you give them the gory details after you promised that nothing in my background would change your love for me?"

"I know I promised, but I didn't think that it would be so disagreeable."

"It's too late anyway, since you've already told your father. That's exactly why I asked you not to tell anyone. It was not your secret to broadcast; it could land me in jail if too many people find out about it."

"I promise it won't get outside the family."

"You said I could trust you. People in love have a right to expect that. Then you turn around tell your father everything you promised not to."

"You're right. But I was scared; I didn't know what to do. I'm very close to my family, I care about what they think, and I've never kept secrets from them."

"Are you saying that you want to tell my story to the rest of your family? Can't you at least wait until after the deal is finalized?"

"Oh no Sam, that would not be possible. Besides, maybe father has already talked to others in the family and…"

"So it sounds like the deal is off," Sam said as she savagely griped the arms of her chair. "How about our relationship, is that off too?"

"I don't know Sam. I just have to wait until after I talk with the family."

"Well I'll be damned! You're going to let the family make your decisions for you? About the building as well as us?"

"Yes Sam, I don't know what else I can do."

"I'll tell you what you can do, Charles. You can take the deal, our relationship, and your family and stuff them all up your royal ass. I'll do the deal myself. I can get along fine without you and your family. I trusted you and you trashed it. I can never forgive you for that!" Sam threw her napkin in Charles' face and ran from the dinning room.

***

Sam was furious as she sped away from the Club toward home. The avalanche of her life was crushing her again, just when she felt she was taking control. Tears were streaming down her face as she parked her car and entered the house. Stopping at the sink for a glass of water she noticed Ramon by the pool and being in a combative mood she rushed out to confront him.

"What the hell are you doing here Ramon? I want you off this property and I want you to stay off!"

"Why you angry? You the one smashed my fucking

face."

"And you're the one who tried to assault me!  Look, I told you that I would pay for your medical bills, but that's as far as I'm going to go.  I don't ever want to see you again.  Do you understand?"

"Don't you want to know why I not tell the Chief what happen?  Maybe you think you bashed that memory from my head, huh?  But I remember, I remember real good, and I get something for it.  Yes ma'am, I get money for my memory."

"What are you talking about, I said that I would pay for your medical bills?"

"See, if you go to jail I not get paid to keep story secret, so I keep you here so I get your money.  Yes sir I want to get your money for what you did to me."

"You attacked me you bastard, I just defended myself," Sam shouted.  "Look bandage face, the minute you told the Chief that you fell and hit your head all by yourself, you lost your leverage.  I won't pay you one dime more!"

"Oh, I think you will missy, I think you will.  I lost power like you say, but I still got memory and I can talk about it all over town.  It won't sound good and some people think about it and wonder.  You can't afford to have your reputation blacked that way. You new money, you don't really belong.  Some old money probably tries finding reason to throw you out right now.  I gave this mucho think, yes sir, I have."

"Oh, shut up you jerk.  I won't pay you a penny for

your memory; nobody will believe a scumbag like you."

"Well I have easy way out for you Sammy girl. Most new money people afraid of losing what they have, and so they buy lots of insurance on their property. I bet you got at least five mil insurance on this place. I not greedy, I no want more than two, three mill. Your insurance will cover that. I can take that back to my country and live pretty good. Now am I being good or what?"

"You are a conniving bastard."

"Yes, I know sweetie, but you know I right and good too."

"Look you dishonest wretch, I know you have a gun. I saw it in your bag in the pool house a couple of months ago. If I find out you tried to shoot me I'll pump you so full of holes you'll be invisible."

"Now why would I try to kill miss money bags? You tell me that."

"The Chief will want to know why you lied to him. Now get out of here."

"I go but think about what I say, but not too long. I talk about my memory. I know lots of ladies who interest in what I say. Adios for now missy."

# *Chapter Twelve*

Chief Watson saw Sam sitting at a table by the fountain in the patio area of the Club that overlooked the tennis courts.  Not seeing anyone on the courts he went to join her.  "Hello Sam, it's nice to see you."

"Oh hi, Chief; it's nice to see you too."

"May I join you?"

"Why of course, I'd be delighted."

"Wednesdays I try to come catch some tennis if possible. In my line of work it's important to stay in shape."

Chief Watson, a handsome black man, was special in Crown City.  He was a Crown City native born to parents who were teachers in the local elementary schools.  He skipped some elementary and high school grades and entered USC on a full scholarship at age sixteen.  He was found to have an unmeasurable IQ and graduated number one in his class while majoring in history and political science and dabbling in psychology, philosophy and tennis.  He entered the Police Academy, without the blessing of his parents, who felt he could do much better. He had a personal passion that the police department was the place he could do the most good for his community. After he had established himself as a competent officer on the fast track, he took time off and received his law degree from UC Berkeley's Bolt Hall.  Returning home to Crown City, he became the youngest to achieve each rank: Sargent, Lieutenant, Captain, and finally Chief of Police. He had the uncanny ability to inspire everyone he came in contact with, especially his competition.

"I brought my tennis stuff also thinking I might catch a game or at least warm up. I need to hit something as hard as I can to get rid of some tension. In the meantime, I love to sit here by the pool and the fountain and meditate. The sound of running water reminds me of my ancestry."

"Yeah, I like it here to. It's very peaceful. We all need to unwind once in a while."

A waiter approached, "Would you care for a drink or something to eat, Chief?

"Hi Toby, I'll join Ms. Mathews with a glass of the house red and a large glass of water."

"Very good sir, coming right up."

Sam finally broke a long awkward silence with the first thing she could think of to say to someone she hardly knew. "Talking about the fountain, I was telling Charles the other day how it serves as a metaphor of life for me."

"Metaphor for life, how so?"

"I won't bore you with all the details. But, in general, the water in the pool represents all the elements of life. The water spouting from a nozzle is an individual life that begins, arcs to its highest point, and then returns to the pool. There, it is randomly mixed with the other water and ready to emerge again as a new individual.

Something like that. Not very profound but I think about it when I sit here. I guess that sounds a little silly, huh?"

"No, actually it's kind of interesting; I hadn't thought of it quite that way but I don't think it's silly. Since you've shared that, I'll tell you something I think about from time to time, not necessarily having anything to do with the fountain of course. Most people think I'm a little strange when I tell them, so brace yourself."

"Ok Chief, I think I can handle it; lay it on me."

"Sometimes I think about where I fit into the universe, where life in general fits. And I think, wouldn't it be interesting if we humans are merely microscopic organisms within the body of this giant, check that, super gigantic organism? What if we're simply tiny little bugs, just like the ones that live within us, that require a microscope to see? We think we're so important and we know so much, but in reality that's all we are--bugs. It keeps me humble."

Smiling Sam responded, "Now that is an interesting concept, Chief. I don't think it's strange, it could be true actually. It reminds me of an old saying that I've often repeated but I'm not sure where it came from."

"By the way, in as much as we're sharing all these innermost thoughts, why don't you call me James. That's my first name, not Chief, ok?"

"You've got a deal Chi—James. Anyway it goes like this.

On the back of a small bug there is a smaller bug to bite him.

And on the back of the smaller bug, a smaller bug,

and so on infinitum."

"What do you think?  They sort of fit conceptually, right?"

"Now that's funny Sam.  That's really funny.  I'll have to remember that one."  The Chief said laughing.

They both sat for a long moment, with smiles on their faces and then Sam studying James's face blurted, "Are you comfortable here at the club James?"

"Yeah.  Why not?"

"Oh I don't know.  Just forget I asked."

"Why, because I'm a black man in an all white club?"

"Yes, I'm sorry.  I can't help but wonder how I would feel if I were the only white in an all black club.  It would be unsettling I imagine."

"It's a blunt question Sam."

"Yes, I know it is.  Forgive me.  It was a stupid question and I'm sorry I asked."

"You're not the first to ask; but it always catches me off guard because I feel quite comfortable here.  My skin is a different color and that causes some people problems and I have to deal with that.  But when they get to know me their reservations usually fade and the skin thing goes away on both our parts.  It's more important for me to be here and demonstrate the things all people have in common than to stay in my 'place' and grumble about being persecuted. I have grown a pretty tough skin over the years."

"I've always been impressed by how well you handle yourself. Everyone I know seems to admire you. You must be a very special person."

"No, not really. I just try to fit in. It's pretty easy to make people understand that it's the person's character that matters, not his complexion."

"But you know better than I perhaps, that where a person finds himself in life is so often determined by chance rather than their capabilities."

After considering the statement James responded, "Yeah, I think that's partly true. I know several guys whose lives were changed by fickle circumstance. Take two guys who do about the same thing that might be unlawful or immoral by the standards of the community. One gets caught and is put into the system. The other is lucky enough to get away with it and just continues his normal life. The first is labeled a bad person, and perhaps put in jail. The other, just as guilty, is considered to be and probably feels like a normal individual. Chance determined the perception and the feeling, not the unlawful act. It can be a strange world."

Almost apologetically Sam confided, "I know, I look back at my own life and recall some of the things that I have done which I have gotten away with. I think about how different things would have been if I had been caught and punished like I should have been. I still think I'm a good citizen and a positive influence on the community, but also how that positive circumstance could have been so easily lost.  Have you ever done something that, if you had been caught, could have changed your journey to be Chief of Police?"

"If I were perfectly honest I guess I would have to say yes, but I'll have to plead the fifth."

"So it's not the act that determines your guilt, but whether or not you get caught.  That's kind of scary."

"I think that's only partly true.  If you recognize that you did something wrong and were just lucky you didn't get caught, you have an opportunity to change the things you do in the future.  If you take advantage of that opportunity, then life doesn't seem to be so haphazard."

"I guess that's true.  If the criminal justice system was reasonable, small deviations from the norm would not be treated so severely that they destroy a persons life.  One can only hope that we have such a system in place."

Before more sharing could go on, Inspector Casey called out from the tennis court, "Chief!  Hey Chief!  How about joining us?"

"Oh, no thanks Casey.  I'm busy sharing war stories right now.  Maybe I'll join you later."

"Come on Chief, bring her with you.  We'll play some doubles till Joe gets here."

"Well, what do you think Sam, you said you wanted to hit something?"

"I don't know James, I haven't played men's doubles

for a while. I don't know if I'm good enough to stay with you guys."

"Well, just come down and hit with us. If you don't feel comfortable we can stop. Deal?"

"Ok, I'll give it a try."

"Great! These guys are pretty good but I think we'll be ok. Casey and I were on the team in high school. Ever since, he's always trying to beat me at something, anything, actually. If you're not comfortable after warming up just let me know."

"Ok!"

"Casey, you're on." James shouted from the table and then he and Sam made their way down to the court.

"Sam this is Sean Casey, you met him the other morning at your place, and this is Ed House. Boys, meet Sam."

Sam, with a big smile replied, "Nice to meet you both."

House responded, "Yeah, how are ya Sam. Can we get started now?" He had disdain written all over his face and Casey just smiled because he thought this might be his opportunity to give the Chief his comeuppance.

After about ten minutes of warm ups everyone seemed pleased with one another and House said, "Ok why don't we play a few games? I don't think Joe is going to show for a while, and the little lady looks like she can play. What do you say James, think you're man enough?"

"What do you think Sam, it's up to you?"

"Sure, how can we refuse a sweet invitation like that?" Sam was boiling inside at House's remark. She always responded well to a challenge and besides, she was anxious to make House eat his words and maybe a tennis ball as well.

"OK, you're on guys," James said and then turning to Sam, "Which side do you like Sam?"

"I'm a little stronger on the forehand side but I like both."

"Forehand it is. Let's give 'em hell."

Chief Watson won the toss and chose to serve first. Before he served he said to Sam, "House has a tendency to hit at the net person until they prove they can handle it, so be on guard."

"OK, but I'm sure he won't try to hurt me," Sam said coyly.

"I wouldn't be too sure about that Sam."

The Chief served well to Casey in the deuce court and no balls were hit to Sam. On the Chief's second serve House sent a screaming forehand return toward Sam at the net. She was not prepared for the speed of the shot and it glanced over the frame of her racquet, hitting her in the chest with a thud.

James took a step toward Sam and said, "Sam, all you alright?"

Sam waved him off as she responded, "Yeah Chief, I'm fine. You warned me." She was a little stunned, but play continued and she quickly regrouped.

Sam got a put away at net on the next point. Then James again had to take a second serve to House who proceeded to slam another blistering forehand toward Sam at the net. This time she was able to get enough frame on the ball to deflect it for a winner and they went on to win the first game with no further problems.

The House/Casey team won game two and Sam lost her first service game. During these games Sam slowly got accustomed to the speed of the game, but on several occasions was barely able to get a racquet on the many balls coming her way. After the third game, with the Chief and Sam down two games to one, they took a break.

During game four nothing out of the ordinary happened, and the House/Casey team came out the winner and led 3-1.

Starting game five James served two aces and a winner on his serve, to lead 40-love. However, he missed his first serve to House again and had to take a second serve. House sent another screamer to Sam at the net. This time, being better prepared, Sam hit it squarely in the sweet spot and sent it directly back at the feet of the incoming House who was unable to return it. Sam's confidence continued to grow as the majority of the opponents shots where directed at her. The harder they came the harder they returned as she scrambled all over the court. It seemed for a while that she was not playing with a partner and she rose to the occasion exclaiming excitedly as the adrenaline powered her game and she became the animal that the occasion required. James tried diligently to enter the rallies but Sam's play and that of her opponents wouldn't allow it. Her team, such as it was, won the next two games making the score 3-3 at the second break and her opponents began to reconsider their strategy.

Following the second break, when the combatants retook their positions, Sam whispered to the Chief, "Ok James, we have toyed with these bums long enough, let's show 'em who's the chief." In the seventh game Sam was able to put a wicked spin on the first serve and it kicked out of Casey's reach for a winner. She then served to House drawing him wide and forcing a weak return, which James put away with no problem. On Sam's next serve to Casey, she again went wide with a spin serve. He was able to get to it this time and tried to place a lob over Sam as she charged the net. She was quick enough to stop, retreat and was about to hit a cross court overhead when she noticed House at the net and she hit a wicked overhead right at him. He was caught off guard and the ball smacked him in the groin with a thump. On his knees he yelped, "Damn—what the hell you doing?"

Sam stared at him for a second and said, "Oh sorry Mouse, I hope I didn't hurt you!"

"House! The name is House, damn it."

"Oh, yes, House, sorry."

Three of the combatants were smiling as they returned

to their positions to continue play; one was frowning in pain. Sam finished the game with an ace at the T, further humiliating the recovering House as she and James improved their lead and they went on to take the set 6-4 and the match was called.

Before going to the net for handshakes Sam jogged to James, planted a kiss on his lips and said, "That was great James, how about if I buy you dinner?"

James was surprised, because they had never done anything socially before. He didn't say any thing for a few seconds.

"It's not a marriage proposal James. It's just dinner. I want to reward you for carrying me."

"Yeah, sure Sam. I miss a lot of dinners at home; that won't be a problem."

"Great. I'm going to take a quick shower and I'll see you in the dinning room in about half an hour, ok?"

"That's fine Sam, I'll do the same. See you in half an hour."

***

When Sam arrived at the dinning room she did not see James so she was seated at a table while she enjoyed her martini and people watched. A familiar menacing voice interrupted he reverie. "My informant said that I could find you here. Don't get up."

Sam stiffened in her chair and turned in the direction of the voice. "Mr. Wolf, how the hell did you get in here?"

"You shouldn't be surprised. I can do anything I want, anytime I want. Getting into this country club was child's play."

"How did you find me?"

"Again, I can do anything I want. Didn't take a rocket scientist. Although, you are just a bonus."

"What do you mean?"

"Well I came here because the money trail for Josh's murder originated here. And low and behold I find you. And you wonder why I think you had something to do with Josh's death?"

"What do you mean the money came from here?"

"Don't play coy with me. Some money bags from here paid to have Josh murdered, as if you didn't know."

"That can't be true," Sam said in disbelief.

"My contacts are everywhere sweetheart. It has taken some time, but this is the place alright."

"So you know who paid for the hit on Josh?"

"No not yet, but I did find you. Maybe you should tell me."

"You are out of your mind. How many ways have I got to tell you, I don't know anything about Josh's death?"

"You'll have to admit finding you here, where the money came from, is quite a rare coincidence."

"I don't believe you. I think that's just part of your

game of trying to intimidate me."

"Yeah, right."

"What did you have to do with my parents' death?"

"Oh yes that was unfortunate. All we wanted to do was scare them a little bit and they panicked. That wasn't my fault."

"Then you admit that you killed my parents." Sam jumped from her seat and attempted to hit Mr. Wolf when his bodyguard grabbed her hand and forced her back to her seat.

"I'm not admitting anything except that it was an unfortunate accident. Now back to the question of the moment, what do you know about who paid for Josh's hit?"

"I don't know anything."

"Then why are you here."

"To get away from you, you idiot!"

"You better come with me so we can have a long talk."

"You better not try to get rough with me."

"Oh yeah why not?"

"I have put together a detailed history of Wolf Enterprises, including completed contracts, off shore accounts, operating procedures, the whole gory details I got from Joshes files. It will go to the FBI if for some reason I don't check in regularly."

"You'll tell me what I want to know by the time I get through with you."

"You can't take that chance, that information would destroy you if it got out. It's my life insurance policy."

"You little tramp, you wouldn't dare spread that information around. It would implicate you as well as me. Let's go." His bodyguard grabbed Sam's arm and pulled her to her feet.

"May I be of assistance gentlemen," James said as he stepped between Sam and the bodyguard and forced him to release his grip.

Before punches could be thrown Sam called out, "Mr. Wolf, I'd like you to meet the Crown City Chief of Police, James Watson."

Mr. Wolf looked startled and said, "Hold on, Tomas." After a few moments of angry starring at Sam and the Chief, Mr. Wolf continued, "Just step aside Chief. You're out-gunned here, and I've got business with this little tramp."

"I could have this place surrounded in minutes Mr. Wolf, I don't think you want to play that game," James said in a confident tone and a steady stare.

Mr. Wolf alternated his study of James and Sam and finally said, "Our disagreement is not settled Sam. We will resume our discussion at another time."

"If you want to press charges, we can take them downtown, Sam."

"Thank you James, I don't think that will be necessary. I think we have reached a stalemate." She then turned and said, "Remember the insurance policy Mr. Wolf; the price for taking me would be extremely high," Sam warned. "And I don't see any reason at all that we need to see one another again. Do I make myself clear?"

"You haven't heard the last of this Sam. My people will be around for a while." Turning to his men, Wolf started toward the exit, "Let's get out of this stinking place."

"This is the last time you will be welcome here gentlemen. Don't try to come back or you will be arrested on the spot," James said in his most authoritative voice.

As Mr. Wolf's entourage left, James took a seat at Sam's table. "What was that all about?"

"He's the father of my late husband who doesn't like to take no for an answer. Thank you for coming to my rescue. I was getting ready to punch 'em out," she said with a smile.

"Well you handled yourself quite well out on the court, I guess you could have handled the situation in here as well, but it didn't look like the odds were in your favor."

"I'm just as glad you stepped in James. Somebody could have gotten hurt." James just smiled and Sam continued, "Back to more pleasant things, the tennis was fun, your friends were pretty good."

"Yeah, those guys are the number two doubles team at the club."

"And I suppose you're on the number one team?"

"Guilty as charged, but you were a wonderful partner. The aggressiveness you showed was amazing. As much as I tried I couldn't get into the rallies. Eventually I just stood there and admired your play. How come I haven't seen you on the courts before?"

"I don't know, must be a timing thing. That was the first time I've played men's doubles in a long time. It took a little getting comfortable but I've always enjoyed hitting the ball hard and taking chances. Just getting the ball over the net has never been my goal. I like to go for winners and not depend on my opponents making a mistake, what's the fun in that? Any way going for winners increases your chance of winning and I like to win. Bet you thought you were in trouble those first few games?"

"House is quite a competitor; kind of nasty, actually." There was silence for some time and then, "I think we need to talk a little more about Mr. Wolf and why he was here."

"There is plenty of time for that James. I've got things under control."

"It didn't look like things were under control."

"Come on James lets talk about something else, ok?"

"How much do you know about Ramon?"

"Oh, not much. He just cleans the pool. What is there to know?"

"First of all, he does own a gun."

"Really?  I thought he said he didn't."

"He did.  Also there is some question whether he is in this country legally—and if he was in the hospital all night following the shooting."

"Hummm.  I can't think of any reason why he might take a shot at me, if that's what you're getting at.  Besides he seemed to be pretty beaten up."

"Yeah, the hospital said he had a concussion, but they thought he was handling it well.  They also said that the blunt shape of his head wound was inconsistent with hitting the side of the pool.  There was blood on his jacket but he refused to take it off.  They thought that was a bit weird but didn't pursue it."

"That does sound suspicious but couldn't it have been there for some time?  The blood I mean.  He can be arrogant at times, but from what I gather the ladies in the area seem to like him."

"That's the story I'm getting too, although 'like' might be a little understated.  Well, so much for Ramon.  I tried to check on your gun permit, but I couldn't find any records for a Ms. Sara Andre Mathews before you came to Crown City."

"Well that's interesting isn't it," Sam stalled and then added, "maybe that's because I changed my name after my husband died and the system just hasn't caught up."

"What name did you have before you changed it?"

"Oh really James, do we really have to go into all this now?"

"We're going to have to deal with it soon because I have been looking into the murder of Mr. Chandler and Carolyn Bennington, and your name popped up."

"You're kidding, how?"

"Someone said that they saw you when the shooting took place."

"Why is that important?  Obviously if I was at the scene, I couldn't have done the shooting, right?"

"You have a point, but it's interesting that a woman with no history just happens to show up at that time. In the Chandler murder investigation, you seem to be a potential piece of the puzzle."

"Well, my husband was here to look at some antique guns which were being offered for sale.  I was just fooling around taking pictures of the crowd.  I was scared to death when the shooting started, but I tried to help Carolyn and Charles after she was shot, you can ask Charles."

"Your husbands name was Wolf, at least that was the name he registered under when you were here, the same as the guy you were just talking to, what's the connection?"

"Really James, you seem to be giving me the third degree, like you thought I was a criminal rather than a friend.  It's making me feel very uncomfortable."

"I'm sorry Sam, there are just so many loose ends where you're concerned.  I'm just trying to tie it all together so that I can keep you out of the formal investigation if I can."

"Well I've lost my appetite."  She rose from her chair and said, "If I'm not under arrest, I'm going home."

"Sam, I'm acting as your friend for the time being, but you've got to help me put this puzzle together."

"I've told you all I can tell you James.  My life has become a mess.  That's all I can tell you now."

"The investigation is continuing," James called after her.  "The next time we talk may have to be down at headquarters, unless you're willing to fill in a few blanks for me."

# *Chapter Thirteen*

Tonight was a rare one for Sam; she had no commitments and decided to treat herself to a long, hot, soaking bath with candles, wine, cheese, and soft music—the works. She hadn't had a long talk with herself for years, and the bath was the perfect location to relax and consider the world and her place in it.

She liked to talk out loud to herself to see how her ideas might sound to someone else. "Here I sit in my warm bath with wine and cheese, in this wonderful house, feeling very smug and self important. It reminds me of the story my dad used to tell. 'Three gentlemen were siting on the patio of a very large house. After drinking, telling jokes, and telling 'war' stories the host shouted, 'I wonder what all the poor people are doing today?' and they all burst into laughter at the rhetorical question. Of course nobody on the patio cared about 'the poor people'; they were just acknowledging how special they were and basking in a feeling of self-importance. Something like I feel tonight—I feel I've really got it made, as if I'm somebody. But unlike the men on the patio sometimes I feel a little uneasy about it. I've done some things that deserve the good life, that's true, but all of the terrible things that I have done along the way keep flooding my mind. I really feel pain in the gut for the bad things I've done; it's much more visceral and powerful than my triumphs are uplifting. If I had been caught for my bad deeds and put in jail, it would have been justified and

I wouldn't be sitting here wondering how to spend the fortune they afforded me. It makes you wonder why things are the way they are and why things turn out the way they do." She then slowly bit through a piece of Jarlsberg cheese, chewed a few times, and washed it down with a sip of Pinot Noir.

"That was a hoot the other day when James said he thought that humans were nothing but bugs in the belly of a giant organism. I can just imagine each bug thinking they were special, with friends, family and probably neighborhoods, towns and countries just like we do. Wouldn't it be something if that's all that we were? Contemplating the dimensions and boundaries of the Universe would be simplified; it's pretty humbling to think of people as just bugs in somebody's belly. I'm more inclined to think that we are special beings in this Universe, more than bugs, but a lot less than most people believe." That last thought brought a smile to Sam's face as she took another sip of wine.

"To me God is a hypothetical construct devised by men to help explain the unknowable, and religion an organization—also devised by men—to collect money to perpetuate itself while keeping women 'in their place'. The myths religious systems promulgate have power by virtue of promising a glorious afterlife for the people who agree with them and the fiery furnace for everyone else. I do think that if there were a God, she wouldn't know any more about a particular person than that person knows about a particular molecule in his liver. A cynical point of view one might suppose, but perfectly logical for someone a little fuzzy from a bit of the bubbly."

"Sometimes I feel sorry for the highest people in religious organizations. They claim to be in communication with God, and doing His biding on the people's behalf. On their journey to that lofty position they must have, at some point, realized that there is no divine insight available to enlighten them, that answers come from within themselves, they are not given to them. What a dilemma for them, poor guys. They must have a profound feeling of guilt when they realize how alone they are, and yet they dress in their funny clothes and tell their followers that they are expressing the word of God. They are caught in a vicious cycle of deceit from which they can't escape if they hope to rise to the top of the house of cards of their own making."

"Their collective guilt probably accounts for the authoritarian nature of religious organizations which compel people to believe as the religious authorities decree, or else bad things will happen. That authoritarianism has caused more destruction of life and property than any other force in human history. It's disturbing that so much of the world's atrocities have been committed in the name of God and religion."

"Wouldn't it be much simpler and cheaper if parents taught their children to treat each other in the same way that they would like to be treated, and to live life as if tomorrow was their last—rather than the church teaching all their conflicting dogma and building lavish cathedrals to impress people? Simplifying the message would make our life and the lives of everyone around us simpler and happier. Oh well I can only dream. Maybe if I prayed to someone that would help. Ha, don't hold your breath!" And she had another sip of wine.

"When I think about the origin of life I think it all started in the 'pool of life' which began as a single chemical reaction at the bottom of the ocean millions of years ago. Unlike the pool at the Club, this pool currently extends around the world with a tiny bit of DNA contained in every person on earth. A random set of genes from the mom and pop creates a new and unique offspring. How and why they got them is probably determined by chance. One hardly needs a divine being for an explanation. Originally the precious chemicals probably combined in the hot lava gases at the bottom of the ocean that emanates from the core of the earth. Scientists say that hundreds of new combinations of compounds are being created every day. So many life forms are down there that they can't be counted. It's not a great stretch to believe that human precursors came from the depths of the Earth's core."

"There is no special purpose for man being here on earth. We just happened, so get over it. But if you follow the thinking of some scientists—that we all came from a single mother—there had to be a father and a whole lot of brothers and sisters humping each other in order to account for the growth of the human population. Maybe that's why there are so many screwed up people in the world; too many close relatives humping each other in the beginning. I don't know how else they got from one mother to where we are today without a lot of familial hanky panky." She marveled at the strangeness of the situation and took another sip of wine and savored the cheese, crackers and soft music.

"The tenure of an individual's physical body is brief, its demise is certain and its ultimate residue insignificant. What little physical remains are left upon a person's death and decomposition, gets re-circulated by the earth, air and water and eventually enters the pool of life in some form. Therefore the only place we go when we die is back to where we came from. For those who want to believe in an after life, the good news is that the half-life of a person's ideas can be infinite. An ideas quality is measured by how long they influence others' ideas. There does not seem to be a place for a soul in the life cycle, although if ideas survive death, that part of you can live forever."

"But I do wonder from time to time if I had been a staunch Episcopalian like Charles and believed in an all-powerful benevolent God, if it would have enabled me to withstand Josh's brainwashing. Would I have stayed married to him after I found out what he did for a living? I don't know the answer to that question, but sometimes I wonder. Clearly my own belief system failed me. Perhaps at times it's better to have an ignorant belief than a reasoned skepticism." Following that disturbing thought Sam had another sip of wine and sat back to consider these great questions and the effect that her personal philosophy has had on her life.

As she opened her eyes from these reveries, she became

aware that there was no music, and the only light she could see was from the candles that decorated the bathroom. She knew that she had left the lights on in the bathroom and bedroom, but now they were all off. The sudden realization startled her. For a time she remained confused because of her fuzzy-headedness resulting from the Pinot Noir; it made sober, critical thinking difficult. She remained in good spirits at first, but as she became more attentive, alarm rose to dominate her mood and trigger fear. "Was Ramon or Mr. Wolf up to dirty tricks?" she thought. After a few minutes she realized that it was more likely that electricity in the neighborhood had gone out. However, she was concerned enough to rise from the tub and slip into her robe.

She cautiously entered the bedroom and worked her way to the window to look out. The street lights and the neighbors' lights were on, as were the lights in the house down the street. She backed away from the window and removed the pistol she kept in a drawer next to her bed. She checked to ensure the clip was full, and thrust it into the handle of her Glock nine-millimeter weapon. The room was shadowed and dimly lit from the candles in the bathroom. Cautiously she made her way to the bedroom door and peered down the hall and stairs. She was still a bit unsteady from the wine, but the adrenaline was now surging.

She felt that she might be over reacting, but wasn't willing to take a chance given the recent shooting and the way her life was going at the moment. She tried the light switch in the hallway. Nothing happened. She crept down the stairs with the pistol in ready position and tried the switch in the living room. Nothing.

Lights in the entire house seemed to be out. She wondered, "Is this just a routine tripped circuit breaker, in which case resetting it would restore power? Or is there something more sinister going on here?" She continued around the living room in a crouched position, continued into the kitchen and peered self-consciously out of the kitchen window into the darkness of the back yard and the pool area. The main electrical box was just outside the back door next to the air conditioner. Sam pondered for several minutes, weighing her options. She hadn't lived this long without being cautious. However, she felt a little silly; the wine may have morphed a routine household breakdown into something apparently hostile. But after the pool house situation with Ramon, the sudden appearance of Mr. Wolf, and being shot at, it was prudent that she be careful. She began slowly to open the kitchen door, then threw the door wide-open and crouched on the floor for several minutes surveying the backyard, gun ready.

She changed her position and direction several times as she darted down the stairs and made her way to the electrical box, thinking, "If I were a gunman I would wait till the potential target were reaching for the electrical box door, providing a stationary target." When she got to the electrical box she crouched behind the air conditioner for several minutes. She had reset the main circuit breaker before and knew exactly where it was located.

She could not reach the box without rising from the

protection of the air conditioner. After waiting briefly, she rose to reach for the box and then fell immediately back to safety. There was silence as she scanned the darkness. She waited several minutes and then faked the same motion again. She waited several minutes more and then cautiously rose, opened the door of the electrical box and reset the main circuit breaker, which had been tripped. The lights in the house and yard came on as she fell again to a safe position.

Sam felt silly, but was still shaking as she walked back into the house and poured herself a glass of water to steady her nerves. As she sipped the water she noticed there was a yellow pad and pencil on the kitchen table. Looking more closely she could see that the pad contained a rather long hand written note.

"Hello Sam, it's been a long time, but I finally found where you live. Nice place, but your security system could be improved. I heard you talking to yourself while taking your bath. I didn't realize you were so concerned with thoughts like those. I'd like to continue the discussion with you some time. By the way, you are very beautiful naked. Now I understand why Josh fell in love with you. But enough of this, I have to go. I'll be in touch. PS: don't worry, I'll be gone when you read this note."

Water from her glass began to spill onto the floor as she trembled and her knees became so weak she sank to the chair next to the table. "Someone was in my house, watched me in the bath, listened to my personal thoughts. He even took time to find the pad of paper in the study and write a long note. He knows Josh?" Tears filled her eyes as the implications of the note hit full force. She lowered her head to her arm on the table and sobbed. Instinct told her that she needed to be with someone. She thought of Charles, but decided he would be of no help. Unconsciously she found herself dialing Chief Watson's number.

"Hello, Chief Watson here."

"Hello Chief, this is Sam Mathews. I am sorry to bother you this late, but something very strange has happened at my house. I wonder if you have the time or would be willing to come over and investigate—as a friend?"

"If you think it's serious I guess I can make the time."

"I don't know if it has something to do with the shooting the other day, but it might. It's not an emergency but I need to show you something."

"I'll be over in a few minutes."

"Thanks James, I really appreciate your help."

***

Sam felt the jitters ebb when Chief Watson arrived. "Hello Chief, thank you so much for coming."

"Sure Sam. What's going on?"

"First of all I want to apologize for the way I acted the other day after tennis. I just felt that I was under siege

175

and panicked."

"It became uncomfortable for both of us. What about tonight?"

"Well I was taking a bath when the lights went out in the house. I went outside to reset the circuit breaker and when I came back into the house I found this sickening note on the kitchen table. Somebody was in my house and they watched me and I didn't know it. I am frightened, but I don't know exactly what to do about it."

After reading the note Chief Watson said, "I can see why you're frightened, Sam. This note and how it appeared is very troubling. Josh was your husband right; Walter Wolfs son?"

"It's a long story. If you have time, let's go into the study and I'll bring coffee." The wine was still influencing her assessment of the situation.

"Ok, but don't go to any bother."

"It's no bother, there is always hot water. I'll be right back."

Chief Watson headed for the study where he found three walls of floor to ceiling bookcases filled with books on a wide variety of subjects. The fourth wall had a fireplace, French doors opening to the patio, and two glass enclosed display cases filled with standard and sawed off-shotguns, automatic pistols of several types and caliber's, sharpshooter rifles with optical and infrared sights, and an assault rifle. The number and variety were impressive. The Chief was particularly interested in the number of tear down weapons and guns capable of accommodating silencers. He thought that was unusual for a private gun collection.

The Chief was thoughtful and stern looking as Sam came into the study with the tray of coffee. "This is quite a collection. Very unusual."

"I told you I had a gun collection, didn't I? Most of them are from my husband's collection. Impressive, aren't they?"

"Indeed." Taking a sip of coffee, the Chief exclaimed, "You've laced this with a lot of Kailua. Tastes great, but I shouldn't be drinking on the job."

"Then think of it as spending time helping a friend who has a problem."

"OK Sam, but this is serious stuff. Your false identity, your association with the Wolf family, somebody shoots at you, and now there's a note from someone who broke into your house. You have a security system, don't you?"

"Yeah, but that didn't seem to slow him down much. Whoever broke in must be pretty sophisticated."

"You're right about that. At first I thought we were dealing with Ramon, but now I'll have to take another look at that. I don't think his knowledge of security systems is sophisticated enough to have bypassed yours. By the way, my guys told me that there is a stranger in town asking questions about you, and I don't mean Mr. Wolf. Before this happened tonight I figured that the questions had to do with your business deals, so I didn't mention it to you before. He wanted to know how long you had lived here, where you came from, where you lived, and things like that. Come to think of it, I'd like to know those things as well." He paused briefly as he looked deeply into Sam's eyes, "Anyway has anyone contacted you?"

"No one has contacted me, except for this note of course. No business partner would pull a stunt like this. I'm probably a little paranoid right now, but under the circumstances, you probably understand. This guy could have been one of Mr. Wolf's people, but I think he would have done more than just leave a note. As you saw, the Wolf clan is not exactly known for finesse."

"Yeah, I'll have to ask the guys more about this other guy." After making a note to himself he continued, "The intruder tonight says that he knew you and your husband before. Does that bring anyone to mind?"

"A lot of people knew Josh and me when we were in college together. We were married for three years while we were in college. He was killed in a hunting accident shortly after our graduation. I never made any lasting friends in college, but I don't think I made any lasting enemies, either."

"The handwriting appears to be a man's, but I'll have some experts examine the note and pencil to see if there are any prints. They should come over and dust the house to see what they can find."

"Thank you for coming tonight, after the way I acted the other day. I'm finally thinking a little straighter. You have a calming effect on me."

"Glad to be of help, Sam. I can understand why you were upset. It was also interesting to have seen your gun collection. It's pretty rare for a woman to have such a substantial gun collection, don't you think?"

"Maybe so, but I think women and men have more interests in common than most people think. The two genders distribute themselves randomly across many emotional and physical continuums. In the middle they're pretty much indistinguishable as I understand it."

"Maybe I'm making too much of gender stereotypes, I know that not all hobbies are gender specific. That reminds me, I heard about your demonstration of strength a few weeks ago at the club, bringing that guy to his knees with a firm grip. It's been the talk of the club women's circuit and most of the women I know are holding you in awe."

"Guess I did get a bit carried away, but I hate strange men being rude and hitting on me. Now that we have the gender thing settled I must resort to my 'feminine' side and say that I am not going to be comfortable here alone tonight. Is there any chance you could send someone by to keep an eye on things?"

"Sure, I can send a patrol car by several times during the night. You have reason to be concerned—but I'm determined to get to the bottom of this."

The thought of the Chief going and leaving her alone

struck Sam unexpectedly hard, and she said in earnest, "James I'm becoming nervous again, I don't know what's come over me. I guess it's just registering that somebody is out to get me and when you leave I'll be all alone in this house. I've been lucky twice now, but I don't know how long my luck will hold out. Everyone sees me as a strong, confident person, but right now I'm feeling pretty vulnerable." Tears welled up in her eyes and she snuggled her head on the Chiefs shoulder.

The Chief was tempted to stay, but after providing a comforting hug he turned saying, "I understand Sam. I'll call for a patrol car right now. I'm sure nothing further will happen tonight. I'll call you first thing in the morning, OK?"

"Sure Chief; I apologize for the jitters. I'll be all right in a little while. Thank you for coming to my rescue so quickly."

# *Chapter Fourteen*

Sam responded to the ringing phone in her house, "Hello, this is Sam."

"Hi Sam. This is Chief Watson. How are you doing today?"

"I'm fine Chief, thanks for checking."

"Can you meet me for lunch at the club tomorrow?"

"Sure James, be glad to."

"I want to bring you up to date on a few things in an informal way."

"Ok, Chief, what's a good time?"

"I thought about one thirty. That way we miss the noon crowd. Is that ok?"

"That works. I'll see you then."

Sam was grateful for any information about the shooter and the intruder. Until recently, things had been going so smoothly that she had begun to feel that her life was back to normal. She had a great house, seemed to be accepted by the right people in town, and her relationship with Charles had been just fine. All of a sudden things were unraveling, and she was willing to do just about anything to get things back on track.

***

When Sam arrived at the club James and his wife were already seated and he rose to greet her. "Hello Sam, thanks for meeting us for lunch. I'd like you to meet my wife Arlisha. Arlisha this is Sara Mathews, better known to her friends as Sam."

"Yes I know, it's nice to meet you Sam. James has told me a great deal about you. All the women here at the Club are happy that you took care of Mr. Tubbs."

Sam said, "Hello Arlisha, I'm happy to know another member of the Watson family," and then she scowled at James.

"Please have a seat Sam. Arlisha has to leave for a meeting down the hall soon, so we drove together." His way of answering Sam's scowl.

"Sam is an unusual name for such a beautiful woman Ms. Mathews. How did you come by it?"

"Your husband thinks 'unusual' should be my middle name," Sam interjected. "It's my initials actually; SAM. My dad got that started years ago."

"How interesting. I don't think that would work for me." Arlisha looked puzzled while trying to figure out what AOW could spell. "Anyway I've got to get going, nice meeting you Sam."

"Glad to meet you too, Arlisha."

"I'll meet you out front about two-thirty, is that ok sweetheart?"

"Yeah that's fine baby." James said as he rose to kiss

her goodbye.

As Arlisha walked away James said, "I thought it would cause less talk if my wife came with me. I hope you understand, it doesn't take much to get the rumor mill working."

"I was a little startled at first, but I figured you had your reasons."

Chief Watson quickly got down to business, "I know I shouldn't be telling you this; it's strictly police business, but if you agree not to spread it around I do have some interesting information."

"Of course James, my lips are sealed."

"We received test results back comparing saliva on the cigarette butts in the bushes at your house and the blood on the side of the pool. They belong to the same person. We're still waiting for the DNA tests from Ramon and we need to do some more checking on the bullet and the gun we found when we searched Ramon's house before doing anything. We want to have an air tight case before we arrest him."

"After going over everything in my mind I thought it could be him. Did you ask him why he did it?"

"Not until after the arrest. Do you have any idea?"

"No not really. I can't picture him as the one who broke into my house though. That seems to be a little too sophisticated for him."

"That's right. The guys found a few fingerprints at your

place, mostly yours and Charles', not Ramon's. Judging from their size, another set seems to be a woman's—maybe your housekeeper. We're still checking. There was a trace amount of powder, usually found on latex gloves, on the door knob, the desk and the pencil so we think he was pretty careful."

At this point, Inspector Casey and another man interrupted Sam and Chief Watson. "Hi Chief. I'd like you to meet Ralph Randle, an old high school buddy of mine. He's just moved here and I told him I'd introduce him around. He wants to talk to you about a civilian job."

"Hello Ralph, nice to meet you. We're always looking for good people. Drop by the office and we can talk." They shook hands and James turned to Sam, "Randle, meet Ms. Mathews."

Smiling, Ralph extended his hand. "Hello Sam, wonderful to finally meet you." He then turned back to James. "I'll drop by the office, Chief. Sorry for interrupting your lunch, but I'm very anxious to meet people because I'm new in town. It can be so lonely when you don't know anyone. I had to threaten Casey before he would make the introductions, so don't blame him. Hope I'll see you again, Sam."

"Mr. Randle. I know it's sometimes hard to get acquainted when you move to a different city. Good luck finding work."

"Thanks Sam, I'm going to do my best. Sorry about the interruption Chief. Hope to see you all again."

The third time Ralph mentioned her nickname, Sam was startled by the realization that no one had said her name was Sam.  She looked quizzically at James; who seemed to read her mind and gave a knowing look and a shake of the head as the intruders walked away.

"That was a little strange, don't you think James?  I mean, he knew my nickname."

"Yeah, I caught that.  He kind of looks like the guy who was asking questions about you a while back.  I guess he could have found out your nickname while he was gathering information.  But the better question is why is he so interested?"

"You think it could be the same guy?"

"He fits the description.  You've never met him before?"

"No.  I thought that was perfectly clear.  A little while ago you were giving me classified information and now you ascribe ulterior motives to me."

"Don't go all paranoid on me now.  Before I was just trying to let you know that I am on your side and that I'm being up front with you hoping that you would respond in kind."

"But I still feel like you suspect me of some grand conspiracy of something."

"What do you expect when you show up in town with no history on record and seem to be related to an international crime family?"

"You must be referring to the Wolf family."

"That's right. We have been investigating the Wolf family since he showed up at the club, but it has been difficult. They really know how to keep under the radar."

"They probably just want to be left alone. Not much different than most families, I imagine."

"We have learned enough about them to think of them as an international crime family. Unfortunately, you seem to be right in the middle of them."

"I regard you as a friend James, but your position as the Chief of Police also makes things awkward."

"I'm working hard to separate the official investigation from our personal relationship, Sam. For anyone else with your background, I would have hauled her downtown, maybe in handcuffs. But I just don't think of you as a suspect. I like you personally and that's what's holding me back. Now off the record, what's your story?"

"Off the record?"

"Yes, for the time being."

"I told you that my husband was a member of the Wolf family. After he was killed, I had a falling out with the family and I was trying to hide out in Crown City until the difficulty could be resolved, that's why I changed my name. I thought this would be the last place they would look for me. For some reason they've got it in their head that I had something to do with my husbands death. Of course, that is completely ridiculous."

"Now that they have found you, what?"

"I have compiled everything I know about the family and stashed it in several places.  If something happens to me, that information will be sent to the authorities.  That's my life insurance policy."

"What is the relationship between the Wolf Family and the Chandler and Bennington murders?"

"I don't know the connection for sure, I can only guess," Sam lied.

"We can force you to tell us everything you know."

"I thought this was off the record, a conversation between friends."

"Damn it, it is, but how can I help you unless I know all the facts?"

"If I tell you everything, I'm a goner."

"The police can grant you immunity from prosecution if the information you furnish brings down the Wolf Family.  That's what I think you should do."

"Yeah, right.  I spill the beans about the Wolfs and someone in the organization takes me out regardless of how hard you try to protect me."

"Very few people in witness protection are ever killed, but I have to admit it does happen once in a while."

"James I'm very fond of you and I don't want to get you into trouble.  Maybe we should just drop the subject right now until I can better determine where I stand with both the police and the Wolfs."

James took Sam's hand in his and said, "I am very concerned about you Sam and I don't wont anything to happen to you."

Sam examined James for several minutes and then said, "I've got to get out of here before I do something foolish." She rose from her chair, reached down and kissed James on the cheek and said, "I hope you find the intruder soon. That will help me decide what to do."

"I'll try to look out for you Sam, but I can't continue to protect you forever."

Sam paused momentarily, smiled warmly at James, then turned to leave. On her way out She noticed Mrs. Chandler and made her way toward her. "Hello Mrs. Chandler. How nice to see you today."

"Hi Sam. Isn't it a lovely day for a celebration?"

"Any day is a good day for a celebration. Your whole family seems to be having a good time out here; this must be a very special occasion."

"It does look that way, doesn't it?"

"By the way I'm in the process of drawing up the paperwork for the Chandler Building. It should only take a couple of days."

Mrs. Chandler seemed surprised and was slow to respond, making the moment a bit uncomfortable. "Uh, I thought you were no longer interested in the building."

"No, on the contrary, I'm very interested and so is Charles. I'm just sorry that it has taken so long."

"Well there must be some mistake. Charles told me that you were no longer interested in the building and would not be a part of the deal. In fact, he said that you wanted nothing to do with the building any longer. He was very clear about that."

"But that's not true. As far as I'm concerned the deal is still on. There must be a misunderstanding some where."

"I'm sorry, dear. Charles brought by the paperwork yesterday. He said you were no longer a partner, and I signed everything. The contract is complete. As you can see we're celebrating. That's what the party is all about."

"I can't believe this, are you sure?"

"I had always thought that you wanted to be part owner of the building. I was surprised when Charles said you had changed your mind, but knowing how close the two of you are, I thought it was a mutual decision. He said there was a good reason for only his buying the building, but didn't explain, just that it was better this way. If that's not the case, I'm very sorry but at this point there's not much I can do."

"Mrs. Chandler this comes as a complete shock. The misunderstanding is not on your part I'm sure. I feel completely betrayed by Charles, but maybe there is a logical explanation. This is something that Charles and I will have to sort out. I'm sorry if I have diminished your celebration, please don't let me interrupt any longer."

"Sam, I..."

Sam turned and hurried from the club as confusion

and anger overwhelmed her.

***

After arriving home she poured herself a glass of wine, turned on Mozart, sat before the fireplace and attempted to put things into perspective by speaking to herself out loud. "Charles has apparently written me off without the courage to confront me—and stolen the Chandler deal in the bargain. All the time that we spent together what was he all about? Does he act one way to my face and another way behind my back? The whole thing makes me sick."

She took another sip of wine and further contemplated the situation. "There are really two issues: first the deception and second the Chandler Building. The way he went behind my back is unforgivable. As far as the building is concerned, I could either let him have it or fight for it. It will take a couple of more days before the deal is legally final I think. It all depends upon how Mrs. Chandler feels about the situation. Charles apparently doesn't want a public fight, but by God that's exactly what he's going to get no matter what it does to my reputation."

Angrily Sam dialed Charles' number.

"Hello, Charles Bennington here."

"Hello Charles this is Sam. We have an issue to resolve."

"Oh really, and what might that be?"

"I talked to Mrs. Chandler and she says you're trying to

steal the Chandler Building out from under me."

"I don't know what you mean 'steal the Chandler Building'. You are more likely to steal something than me."

"You told her I was no longer interested in the deal and had her sign papers under false pretenses. I'm not going to let you get away with it."

"You're a little late Sam. Everything is signed, sealed and delivered. Besides I don't think you want everyone to know about your sordid past; and I don't think Mrs. Chandler would want someone like you to own her building."

"You are treacherous as well as dishonest. Let me tell you something. I'm a much better person than you are, and Mrs. Chandler knows that now."

"Name calling won't help anything. Anyway, be realistic, you don't have legitimate financing without me and I don't intend to have you as a partner."

"Yes, that is now very clear. You didn't have the guts to talk to me about it first. You said your love was unconditional, but you couldn't even be honest about that. You took what I told you, and then stabbed me in the back even though I only did it to protect your life. You don't even know what love means, I really feel sorry for you. I'm putting you on notice right now mister. No matter what you say about me, you are not going to get away with stealing the Chandler Building."

"Look Sam, you don't have a chance in the world of

fighting me. Just get on with your little life, and let things be before I expose you for what you are."

"Yes, you'd like that wouldn't you? Prepare to get dirty, Charles. It's your word against mine; I'll take my chances." She slammed down the phone and trembled with rage. She fumed for several minuets as she finished another glass of wine.

Moments later, still filled with anger, she made another call. "Hello, Mrs. Chandler's residence, who may I say is calling?"

"This is Ms. Mathews, may I speak with her please?"

"Just a moment please."

"Hello Sam how nice of you to call. I was about to call you anyway. I'm having a group of friends over tomorrow about ten o'clock and wanted to know If you could join us?"

"I really appreciate your invitation, Mrs. Chandler. I would like that, but I need to talk to you about the Chandler Building."

"Yes, I thought you might. Why don't you come about nine-thirty and we can talk privately before all the others arrive. Is that alright?"

"Of course Mrs. Chandler. Thank you. I'll see you tomorrow."

After hanging up the phone, Sam angrily threw her empty wineglass into the fireplace, smashing it into tiny shards. The results closely resembled her life at the moment, and spawned doubts about her ever being able to put things back together again. Did she have the strength to start over one more time? Her feelings of hopelessness sat heavily on her shoulders, forcing her to lower her head onto her arm resting on the table, her burden too heavy to face.

# *Chapter Fifteen*

It was difficult to wake up and face the new day—self-doubt almost kept Sam in bed. She knew from past tragedies that directly attacking problems was her only salvation, but it was tough. She resolutely rose, showered, dressed and began her drive to Mrs. Chandler's house. Mrs. Chandler opened the door and said, "Hello Sam, so glad you're here. Please come in."

"Thank you Mrs. Chandler. I appreciate your invitation; it gives me an opportunity to apologize for the scene I made at the Club yesterday."

"Oh don't be silly dear, and please call me Pauline. Let's go into the study for a few moments; nobody else is here yet."

"This is our monthly coffee for a group of 'good old girls'. Most of us have been doing business together one way or another for a long time. We try to counter the 'good old boys' and help balance the playing field in town. We share mutual interests in Crown City, and discuss how it's being run," Pauline confessed as they entered the study.

"Oh really I wish I had known about the group, it sounds like something I would be interested in," Sam replied.

"I hope that you will feel a part of the group and join us when you can. It's nothing very formal, we just meet at each other's homes and talk about what's going on around the city and take action when we feel it's necessary.  Over the years, I think we have made a difference."

"That's very gracious, Pauline.  I'm looking forward to meeting the group.  It's the kind of thing I have missed since moving here.  And the timing is perfect; I would love to get into local issues that have purpose."

"I'm happy to hear that Sam.  I did want to talk to you about the misunderstanding concerning the Chandler Building.  I've been doing some checking, and things don't seem to be quite like Charles indicated.  I'm sorry that I didn't contact you before signing the contract but I had no idea that there would be a problem.  My children and I have been so eager to make the sale that I'm afraid we acted hastily."

"There is nothing to forgive, Pauline.  I probably would have done the same thing, given the information you had at the time.  I don't know exactly what Charles told you about me, but regardless, it was never my intention to give up the Chandler Building.  It's such a beautiful building that if possible I'd still like to purchase it, even without Charles."

"I was hoping that would be the case.  You always seemed to love the building as much as Winthrop and I did.  I could feel your appreciation of its character and charm, more than Charles ever showed.  I think the Bennington family wanted the building just because we had it.  That's why I was so pleased when you said that you were interested in it in the first place. I have a call into our corporate lawyer to see if there is a way that the contract can be rescinded. I just hate to be deceived."

"Charles will not be happy if you try to break the contract. He'll probably have a lot of nasty things to say about me. I admit that I have done some things in the past that I'm not proud of—things that I wish I could amend now with the benefit of maturity. I can't alter my history, but I have learned from it. I have changed quite a bit since coming to Crown City."

"I, and the group, have kept an eye on you since you came to town, and we like what we have seen. As for your past, all of us have done a thing or two in our youth that we'd hope would not come to light; so you're not alone. I don't expect you to be perfect; none of us are."

"Thank you for saying that. I promise to treat the building with respect, and try to bring it back to its original luster. I owe that to you and your late husband," Sam realized that she had almost revealed to much about her involvement with Pauline's husbands death and hurried back to the main topic. "I can put my hands on about five mil for the down payment and the necessary refurbishing. I need to find financing for the rest. I expect that will be more difficult now. Charles will make sure of that. But I am confident that if I work at it hard enough, I will be able to make the financial arrangements."

"If you have collateral, our group may be able to help you find the financing."

"That's a generous offer, Pauline. I'll have my

accountant send you all the financial statements you need. I hope we can work things out."

"Good. I'll have my lawyer check to see how we may be able to invalidate the contract with Charles. Often we think it may be too late, but we find out otherwise."

Just then, Sam's cell phone rang and she recognized Charles' phone number. "I'm sorry Pauline, it's Charles. I better find out what kind of mischief he's up to now. I'll make it brief." Turning away she said, "What do you want Charles?"

"Sam, thank God I got you! I'm in trouble and you're the only one who can help me. Please don't hang up; this is a matter of life or death."

"Oh please, Charles; tone down the melodrama. What kind of trick are you trying to pull now?"

"It's no trick Sam. If you don't come down to the office right now I'm a dead man."

"What makes you think I give a damn? Since you screwed me over with the Chandler building, I don't care what happens to you."

"Oh God, Sam, please don't let me down. You're the only one who can handle the situation. You have to come down here right now or you will be responsible for my death."

"What the hell are you talking about?"

"You're the only one who can make this predicament go away."

"If you're in serious trouble call the police. They can do a lot more than I can."

"He won't let me do that. He only wants you."

"Who are you talking about?"

"I can't tell you that, he only want's you. If anyone else comes he said he would kill me. Please Sam this is not a trick. I'm begging you, get down here fast." The line went dead.

Pauline saw that Sam had begun to shake. "Not bad news, I hope?"

"Charles says it's a life or death matter and he needs me at his office right now. He seemed to be in a panic, so I feel obligated to see what's going on."

"Oh my, he's such a scoundrel," Pauline interjected.

"Please give my apologies to the group. I did so much wish to meet them all. Maybe another time?"

"Of course my dear they will understand. If Charles is pulling a fast one, you let me know. There will be hell to pay."

"Thank you Pauline, I'll let you know what this is all about."

***

On the way downtown, Sam simmered with anxiety, fear and suspicion. She knew that Charles was distraught, he wasn't a talented actor, so the fear and panic in his voice had to be real. She wondered who else was there, why Charles was so afraid, and what role she would play in the drama.  When she got to Charles' office building she hurried to the elevator and ascended to his floor.

She slowly turned the doorknob to Charles' office; then flung the door wide open, and stood silently in the hall.

Charles called out, "Is that you Sam?"

"Yes—what's going on in there?"

"Thank God you've come; this asshole said he's going to shoot me."

"Come in Sam, you in no danger, but I shoot your boyfriend if you no come up with more money than that damn insurance company pay."

Sam cautiously entered the office to find Ramon with his gun aimed at Charles.  "Is that what this is all about? You want more money?"  She was actually relieved that it wasn't one of Mr. Wolf's henchmen.

"Yeah, I want money from you."

"You're damn lucky you got as much as you did. Falls around the pool don't usually pay fifty thousand dollars."

"We know what happen in pool house, don't we Sam. I need money to get out of town.  You give me, or I blow this guy's head off."

"Chief Watson said he had evidence that you tried to shoot me.  Is that why you are in a panic now?"

"I don't know nothing about Watson.  I just need

money."

"Good lord Sam, if all he wants is money, give it to him. You've got plenty."

"Sorry Ramon, the insurance settlement is all you're going to get. Now put the gun down and I'll let you walk out of here. If you do that now, no charges will be brought. Do you understand?"

"Yeah, I understand you cheap after what you did. I kill your boyfriend if you not give me more money." As he shouted he lunged for Charles and twisted his arm behind him and put his gun to the side of his head. The distraction allowed Sam time to retrieve her gun from her thigh holster. As Ramon came to a set position, behind the restrained Charles, he found Sam's Glock nine-millimeter aimed at his forehead.

"Ramon you don't understand what you are dealing with. You saw me in action at the pool house, but now I have a gun on you. If you don't want to die today put down the gun and walk out of here."

"Good lord Sam give him the damn money, I beg you. Please give him the money."

"Sorry Charles, that's not going to happen. Look Ramon, I care less for him than I do you and that's less than zero. You can go ahead and shoot the jerk and then I'll shoot you. It's to my advantage to get rid of both of you anyway. If you continue to hold a gun to his head I will have to kill you."

"Put gun down or I shoot this mother fucker. I swear

I will!"

"This is not a game Ramon.  You have to decide if you want to die today.  If you don't, put the gun down and walk out of here, right now."

"You're just a dumb woman, you don't shoot me."

Charles interrupted saying, "God no, Ramon; she's no ordinary woman she's a hit woman.  She goes around shooting people for money.  It would be easy for her to shoot you.  You better get the hell out of here."

"I don't want to shoot you Ramon, but if you don't do as I say, I will."

"Come on missy, just give me the money," Ramon begged.  "Then I leave town.  That's all I want.  I just want money."

"Just give him the money Sam; I'll pay you back.  I'm begging you here.  Nobody needs to get hurt.  Just give him the money."

"It's gone too far now.  He either leaves or dies, one or the other.  Make a choice Ramon.  I'm going to count to three, and then I'm going blow your head off.  The first shot goes right between your eyes…..One."

"You lie, you don't got the guts to shoot me."

"Two."

Sam lowered herself to a semi crouch position and moved her left hand to support the gun in her right hand.  Her lips opened to say three, and as Ramon saw her tongue slip between her teeth, he shouted, "Ok, ok, ok, I give."  He lowered his gun and pushed Charles to the floor, and glared at him and Sam for a moment and said, "Cheap bitch."  He then turned and started walking toward the door with the gun still clutched in his hand, which hung resolutely by his side.  As soon as Charles saw Ramon's back, he grabbed the phone and started to dial, shouting, "The police will get you, you bastard!"

Sam shouted, "Charles you idiot, he still has the gun!"

Ramon whirled and fired, hitting Charles in the shoulder and then turned the gun on Sam.  She shot before Ramon could fire, the bullet striking him mid forehead.  He was dead before he hit the floor.

Sam walked slowly to Ramon and checked for a pulse; there was none.  She then went to Charles, who was whimpering in pain but did not seem to be mortally wounded.  She moved to the phone and dialed 911.  "This is Sara Mathews, there has been a shooting at 231 East Walnut, office 642.  One man is dead another one is wounded. Send an ambulance immediately."

"Yes ma'am, they're on the way."

Sam then dialed again.  "Hello, Chief Watson's office how may I direct your call?"

"Hello this is Sara Mathews.  This is an emergency.  I need to speak to Chief Watson now."

"Very good ma'am, I'll connect you directly."

"Sam, what's going on?"

"Hello Chief. There has been a shooting in Charles' office. Ramon shot Charles and I shot Ramon. Ramon is dead. Charles should be ok but I need your help. I already called 911."

"All right Sam. Sit tight; I'm on my way."

The Chief, the black and whites as well as the ambulance, all arrived about the same time. Chief Watson surveyed the crime scene briefly, as the paramedics began to examine the victims.

A paramedic--pointing to Ramon--said, "This one's dead. The other one is still alive but we've got to get him to the hospital stat; he's in shock."

"Ok take him away. Leave the other one for a while so the crime scene team can complete their investigation."

Meanwhile Sam sat in a leather chair with her head thrown back and eyes closed, the gun still clutched in her hand.

Chief Watson approached, and with a gloved hand, removed the gun from her hand and placed it in an evidence bag, then gave it to the uniformed officer standing to his side. Sam did not react. He then knelt beside her chair, "Sam, are you alright?"

She slowly opened her eyes and said, "Hello James. Tell me all this didn't happen."

"First you'll have to tell me you're version of what happened."

After taking a deep breath Sam replied slowly, in a

barely audible tone, "I got a call from Charles that he was in trouble and needed me. When I got here Ramon had a gun on him demanding that I give him money. I refused, and after a standoff Ramon started to leave. As Ramon was leaving, Charles grabbed the phone and started yelling that he was calling the police, so Ramon turned and shot him. Then I shot Ramon when he tried to shoot me. It was a bang, bang situation, strictly self-defense."

"Will Charles verify your story?"

"Well of course, that's what happened."

"Well if Charles verifies your story, we can put this to bed pretty quickly. But regardless, you'll have to come to the station to make a statement. You can call your lawyer from there."

"You mean I've got to go into the system? Isn't there any other way?"

"I'm afraid not Sam. For your own protection everything has to be done by the book. There will probably have to be a hearing later to sort thing out."

"I know you're right James. I'll do what I have to do. Thank you for being a good friend." Sam slowly allowed Chief Watson to lead her down to the police car on their way to headquarters.

# *Chapter Sixteen*

Sam swung her car into an angled parking spot in front of Julienne's—an upscale sidewalk café on the edge of Crown City. She located Mrs. Chandler sitting at a linen covered table and waved. "Hi, Pauline, it's nice to see you. Thank you for meeting me here. It's my favorite place for lunch. The Club gets a little boring sometimes."

"Hello Sam, it's nice to see you. I'm pleased that you finally called. I was concerned about you."

"I apologize for not returning your calls. I went to the Bahamas after the hearing, trying to forget the shooting and the rest of my troubles. When I got back, I needed time to get readjusted so that I could face people again. I'm one of those who seeks seclusion when wounded."

"Oh I understand perfectly Sam, my husband was like that. I'm more of a people person myself. I want other people to share my misery."

"Thank you for being so kind Pauline. I think I'm now ready to share my misery."

"It was a shame that the situation went to a hearing, Sam. Most of us knew the shooting was self-defense. Charles' loss of memory, because of being shot, made things less obvious to the Judge, I guess."

"Yes, that was quite a shock to me as well. But, to be honest, I guess one night in jail and a hearing is not an unreasonable burden under the circumstances. I hope things have been well for you while I was gone?"

"In general, things are fine. You were the one our group was concerned about. I hope you know that the girls and I are here to help ease your re-entry. We are just waiting for an invitation."

"Thank you Pauline, that's a great comfort and I appreciate it more than you know. I'm just feeling my way back right now."

"May I help you ladies," the waitress inquired.

"I'll have a glass of iced tea, thank you."

"Very good ma'am, and you?"

"A glass of lemonade please."

"Thank you, I'll be right back."

The women sat silently trying to find a way to restart the conversation. Finally Sam awkwardly asked, "Are the kids handling their money from the sale of the Chandler building as well as you had hoped?"

"That's one of the main things I wanted to talk to you about. I guess you haven't kept up on things around town during your hiatus, but actually the sale of the building was never completed."

"Really, what happened?"

"First Charles had a devil of a time getting himself together after the shooting. You know he had a collapsed lung and was in the hospital for about two weeks with his wound infection, all the while trying to deal with his loss of memory."

"Yes, he had just gotten out of the hospital for the hearing. But I left town shortly after that and have not kept up."

"Well after getting out of the hospital, he kept taking pain killers and started drinking pretty heavily and just went kind of crazy."

"I'm sorry to hear that, it sounds so out of character for him. He always seemed to be so in charge of things."

"Well a lot of that was outward appearances. I think the family made more of his decisions than anyone thought. Anyway, after he went off the deep end, the family became so upset with him that they refused to support his financial decisions until he got his addictions under control. When he failed to recover on their schedule, they stopped backing the purchase of the Chandler building."

"I'm surprised that the family would turn their backs on Charles. That made it doubly tough on him. No wonder he lost control."

"Yes, we were all surprised about that. But when he ran off to Vegas and married some stripper from the local bar, the family got the marriage annulled and forced him into a rehab center. The escrow ran out on the contract and the final papers were never signed. So the building is still mine."

"Poor Charles. I had no idea that it was so rough for him. What's his situation now?"

"He's running around town rather aimlessly. For a while, his erstwhile girlfriend/wife lived with him, but things got so bad that the bimbo just up and left town. The family gave her some money for the annulment, so at least that's taken care of. It's all quite sad."

"I guess it's like they say, no matter how bad you think your life is, somebody has it worse. I feel badly for him."

"A lot of people do, but there are some who feel he got what he deserved. After he got out of rehab the family saw to it that he continued with the counseling and I believe he is just about recovered and back to normal."

"I'm amazed. It's hard to think of Charles not being completely in control of himself."

"I've got something else for you to consider when you are ready."

Again another long silence while Sam sipped her lemonade and tried to visualize Charles out of control. Finally, "Ok Pauline, what other news do you have?"

"I hope this will be good news, Sam. The Chandler building is still for sale as I said. The notoriety of its former sale dampened the enthusiasm of would-be buyers I think. But I want you to buy it if you're still interested." She paused briefly and then went on. "Before you say anything you must know that we're willing to offer a very fair price to keep it in local hands. The girls and I are able to take back a silent second if you are the buyer. Now isn't that good news?"

"Well I guess it's both good and bad news. I know you

wanted to sell long before now so that can't be good news for you. And while I am still interested, I'll probably need some more time to assess my situation—both financially and emotionally."

"Yes, I realize that. You'll have all the time you need to think it over. There's no hurry. No one is beating down the door for that building; even though I think it is a wonderful opportunity. Take your time."

"You are just full of information to keep me occupied. Thanks a lot."

"Yes I know, forgive me. But right now I have another meeting and I've got to run. Call me when you have made a decision or for any other reason, alright?"

"Thanks, Pauline. I appreciate all the news. You have given me a lot to think about."

"Take whatever time you need to consider the offer. Just remember that we are on your side and would love to work with you. See you soon I hope."

Sam rolled all the information around in her mind. Charles' story was very sad, but the Chandler building had always fascinated her. She wondered if she was ready to take on such a responsibility at this time. Deep in thought, she didn't respond to her name being called until she felt a hand on her shoulder.

"Ms. Mathews, are you in there? Hello Sam!"

"Oh, a, sorry, a, hello."

"Ralph Randle. You remember, I met you and Chief

Watson at the club a while back. I was new in town and looking for work?"

"Oh, oh yes, Mr. Randle. I was lost in thought. Yes, of course I remember. How are you?"

"I'm doing fine Ms. Mathews. May I join you or are you expecting someone?"

"Yes, please do sit down."

"I understand that you have been out of town for some time and out of touch with happenings around town."

"Yes, I was just catching up with Mrs. Chandler a few minutes ago. She tried to bring me up to speed. I hope you have been well, Mr. Randle."

"Please, can I get you to call me Ralph?"

"Yes of course…Ralph."

"May I call you Sam?"

"Sure, you seem to have done that for some time anyway, what's up?"

"I don't know, it's kind of hard finding a good paying job in this town. I've just been doing odd jobs, trying to keep my head above water."

"Nothing panned out with the Chief?"

"Not anything that made me happy. I've been thinking maybe I could go into business for myself."

"Oh that's interesting. What kind of business?"

"Maybe the kind of business that you and Josh were into."

Sam was shocked at the mention of Josh's name. She sat silently for a moment just looking at Randle. Then, with a puzzled look on her face, she asked, "How do you know Josh?"

"Oh yeah, because you have been away I didn't get a chance to tell you anything about myself. It turns out that Josh and I are—a—were distant cousins. We talked several times while he was in college and he told me a lot about you. I saw you a few times, but there just wasn't the opportunity to meet you at that time. After he died I tried to find you, to give my condolences, but you were hard to find. It wasn't until we met at the club that I found you."

"I'm sorry the search was so difficult. A card to my school address should have done the trick, don't you think?" Sam scolded.

"Yeah, that makes sense. But, you know people do stupid things sometimes. Anyway now I can tell you that I am very sorry for your loss in person."

"Thank you for the belated condolences. You mentioned something about going into business, what did you have in mind?" As soon as the words came out Sam knew she had made a mistake by re-opening the taboo subject.

"You know what kind of business. The kind that you and Josh did most of the time you were in college."

Sam settled on the Clinton strategy—denial, delay,

denial, delay—and slowly responded, "I'm sure you must be mistaken. Josh did his thing and I did mine."

"Well me being Josh's second cousin and all, we were fairly close."

"Really, I don't remember him mentioning you."

"Be that as it may, during a hunting trip with him, he had a little bit too much to drink and let a few things slip. He made me promise not to tell anyone. He seemed to think that if I did, my life would be in danger. He actually let me come along on one of his 'business' trips before you became involved. After that the subject was strictly taboo."

"That's interesting. What did you do on this trip?" She continued to inadvertently ensnare herself in the web of this unwanted conversation.

"I think you know what I did, but just for the sake of conversation, I served as a lookout as he shot someone."

"Oh, my god. You must be joking. Josh would never do anything like that." Sam feigned surprise, and she looked at Randle as if he had insulted her.

"Ok, I'll go along. During his drinking binge he gave me some tips about how it was done and how he first found out that his family was into the murder-for-hire business. He said because I was sort of part of the family he could do that. When he sobered up and I told him that he had spilled his guts to me, I thought he was going to kill me. That's when he swore me to secrecy for my own good."

"And you are telling me this bizarre fantasy because?"

"I've tried to do a few things on my own but have never developed the contacts and the secrecy techniques that you need to get into the really big money. The potential clients do an Internet search for you and your accounts and if they can find out who you are they are not interested. I got to know a few guys in the business and learned their techniques but I could never get over the hump. That's why I looked you up."

"You tell a very fanciful story Ralph. Maybe you should write a book. The suspense market is hard to crack, but with your vivid imagination you may have a chance."

"Cut the sarcasm Sam. I don't know if you're still in the business, but I know you still know the business and I need some more expertise. I tried a solicitation a couple of times, but I didn't know how to respond when somebody tried to contact me."

"Like I said, you have a vivid imagination; however, I will not listen for one more minute to your preposterous assertions. If you don't leave now, my first stop will be the police to let them know what you're up to."

"Well that's not very gracious of you Sam. Anyway here's the deal; I want to go into business with you. I would go on all the trips and take care of the hits. You wouldn't have to do any of that. You would be the administrator, taking care of all the advertising, responding to and accepting all contracts, setting up accounts and all the security procedures. We would split the proceeds fifty-fifty and you would deposit my share into an off shore account.  We wouldn't even have to see each other if that's the way you would like to play it. What do you say?"

"Your proposal is meaningless, I don't have the slightest idea what you are talking about and I don't want to have anything to do with you," Sam said as she started to rise.

"Wait, if for any reason you are not satisfied with my performance you can stop at any time just by not contacting me.  With Josh's security procedures in place no one will ever know about our deal and there will be no way I can implicate you if I get caught or killed.  Now that is a safe deal for you.  How can you go wrong?"

"Good afternoon Mr. Randle.  I think you are out of your mind."

# *Chapter Seventeen*

Sam anxiously waited as her uncle Ernie emerged from his cab in front of the Chandler building.  He had a full head of gray hair and a burley body that was unbowed by the hard labor of his profession.  As he bounded quickly to her she said, "Hi Uncle Ernie, it's so nice to see you again.  It's been a long time and I've missed you."

A very broad smile reflected his joy of seeing his 'adopted son" again (He had always treated Sam as one of his "boys").  "Hi, sweetheart, it was great to get your call.  I thought you had forgotten your favorite uncle."

"No way, Uncle Ernie.  You've always been in my thoughts.  I just needed to hole up a while and lick my wounds."

They gave each other an affectionate hug during which Sam replayed in her mind the summer months she had lived with Uncle Ernie and Aunt Mary during her high school years.  She went to work every day with Ernie at the various construction sites his company was responsible for.  He taught her to read blue prints and estimate jobs as well as how to carry bricks and lumber and other manual chores including drywall application.  As she became more skilled, she grew tall, strong and tanned, performing all tasks just like "one of the boys".

Uncle Ernie treated Sam like the son that he and Aunt Mary could never have.  They wanted her to join his construction company after she graduated from high school and work toward an eventual partnership. Ernie and Sam shared a love of design and architectural detail, as well as the effort and skill it took to make it all happen. They became each other's best friend. Sam's parent's convinced her that it would be better for her in the long run if she graduated from college before joining her uncle's company. While later, she was glad that she had gone to college, it was a tough decision at the time.

She studied architecture and economics in college and planned to join Uncle Ernie when she graduated. Then, of course, she met Josh and her entire perspective changed. After all that happened to her in college and after, she was delighted to resurrect her relationship with Uncle Ernie and looked forward to working with him on the restoration of the Chandler building.

After their emotional hug Sam became more somber. "I appreciated your stepping in when my parent's died; it probably saved my life. I should have kept in touch, but I was trying to survive one day at a time and not put you in danger by getting in touch."

"Everybody lost contact with you for a while, but I figured that when you were ready you would call. It was a sad time. We laid your mom and dad to rest in Rose Hills. Lots of their friends turned out to bid them good bye. I was so happy to finally get your call. Since your Aunt Mary died things have been pretty lonely. But anyway, it's good to be here now."

"Thank you so much for doing all that for me. I should

have been there I really feel bad about it."

"Don't worry about it, everything turned out ok." They embraced in a gigantic bear hug after which they go down to business.

"Things are much better now and I'm thinking of buying this building and converting it into retail space, professional offices and lofts. I had such fun the summers I spent with you on the construction sites during high school and I think you and I would be perfect partners to oversee the restoration. What do you think?"

"Well she's a beauty alright. She needs a little cleaning and restoration of all that ornamentation, but that would be about it. My company could handle that with no problem. I can't think of anything I would like better than to work with you again. Then maybe I could talk you into taking over the business some time in the future. The years are creeping up on me and there is no one better I would trust to carry on."

"How about if first we complete this job, and then talk about the future." She reached up and kissed him on the cheek. "I'm so glad this project interests you."

"Me too." His smile was as broad as a river. "We'll let the future take care of it's self."

"Ready to take a look inside? The interior will be the difficult part of the project."

"Good, I would like to bring the beauty back to this faded star."

"This has always been one of my favorite buildings. When I first moved to Crown City I used to come and sit in the lobby and just look around. Everywhere I looked there was something interesting or beautiful—the marble floors, rare wood paneling, statuary niches, and the gigantic crystal chandelier—even though I've seen it dozens of times, it's still special. Every time I come here, I'm impressed by the artistry and the workmanship. I marveled that an architect so many years ago could create something so special. That was before the neighborhood went down hill and most of the building had to be shut down." As she spoke her gaze flowed lovingly around the ornate lobby.

"Yeah, I see what you mean. How do you see changing things on this level," referring to the first floor.

"I see retail space here. The exact nature will be determined by who the retailer is. I think an up-scale clothier, either men's or women's, would fit without major modification."

"Hmm, do you think the neighborhood could sustain something like that?"

"I think if we can get the professional offices and the lofts on the upper floors filled, the right business would beat a path to our door. We need to do the upper floors right and get lease commitments before we finish the bottom, anyway."

"The structure of the building looks strong enough and shouldn't require too much retrofitting." He reassured. "We'll have to make sure we meet all the new codes, especially on the foundation, then start at the top and work our way down. Let's take a look at what's upstairs."

"Ok. I'm happy the elevators still work." The ornamented iron grille door opened as she pushed the button. "We may have to put in some new motors, pulleys and cables, but I don't want to change the cars themselves, they are wonderful."

After spending a couple of hours touring the Chandler building, Sam and Uncle Ernie went to a nearby restaurant for lunch and to discuss the feasibility of purchasing and renovating the building.

A waitress approached and asked, "What will it be folks?"

"I don't know about you Uncle Ernie, but I'll start off with a double martini on the rocks and think of something to eat later."

"That sounds good to me."

"Very good, I'll be right back with your drinks."

"Well, what did you think of the building?"

"Like I said before, she's a beautiful old lady, and I think we can handle the job. There is a whole bunch of figurin I have to do before I can give you numbers and a timeline. I still have questions about the neighborhood, but you know more about that than me. Let me work up the numbers, then we can make the final judgement."

Sam was like a little girl at Christmas time and could scarcely contain her enthusiasm. "That works for me!

I know we can make it work and I really want to do it. I have missed you so much, and too many unfortunate changes in my life have happened since the last time we were together. I will spare you the details now, but maybe later when the time is right you will hear my whole sorry tale."

After they had finished lunch and Uncle Ernie was preparing to leave, Randle interrupted them. "Hi, Sam, before you leave can I have a few words with you?"

"Damn it Ralph, are you following me around or what. This has got to stop. I don't have anything to say to you."

"What's going on here Sam?  Is this guy bothering you?"  Ernie worked his way between Sam and Randle, prepared for a tussle if necessary.  "Give me the word and I'll kick his ass up between his ears."  The determined look on his face displayed the desire to smack the younger man, even though he did not match up well physically.

Reaching out with her hand, Sam restrained Ernie. "He is a pain in the butt Uncle Ernie, but it's not anything I can't handle, though I'd like to see someone beat the crap out of him sometime."

Ernie stood with his broad shoulders squared to Randle, eyes ablaze and jaw and fists clenched, when he said, "Just give me the word and I'll drop this guy like a rock."

"No, it's OK.  It's not something you should worry about," Sam reassured him.

A little disappointed Ernie said, "If you're sure things

are ok, then I think I should hit the road. It's going to be pretty late by the time I get home anyway. You sure you're OK?"

"Yes, Uncle Ernie, everything is ok. It was wonderful spending time with you again and I really hope we can make this work."

"I'm sure we can. I'll be counting on working with you over the next couple of years. Bye, love." As he left he turned to scowl at Randle letting him know that he was annoyed that he had been deprived the pleasure of smacking him around.

"I'm pressed for time Mr. Randle. What is it this time?"

"Well, it's been a couple of days and I'm anxious to get started on our adventure together."

"There is no adventure and there will be no together of any kind, I thought I made that clear."

"Look Sam I'm getting tired of your denying everything. I know what I know from Josh as well as your drunken boyfriend. I spent considerable time with Charles at the local strip club, talking and getting smashed. He told me what you told him about your past. So don't keep trying to deny the whole thing."

"Seems you have been busying yourself with my business for some time as well as listening to drunken stories. Now that's going to stop, or there will be consequences."

"Oh wow, what are you going to do, shoot me? Look,

my hands are shaking I'm so scared!"

Irritated, Sam retorted, "I said I don't want to have anything to do with you, and that's the way it's going to be. Now leave."

Randle continued his verbal attack without hesitation. "Look I can make things very uncomfortable for you in this town by confirming all the stories that Charles told me about you. All I want is your expertise; I'm going down the tubes without it. I intend to get it with or without you permission." Randle's tone and posture were menacing.

"That sounds like a threat, Randle. Do you think it's wise to aggravate someone that you're accusing of being in the murder-for-hire business?" Sam shot back.

"Look I'm in a bind and I need your administrative know-how, that's all. I know everything there is to know about getting to people on a hit list. It wasn't a problem getting into your place, and I can do it anytime I want."

"You bastard; so you're the one who left the note. I'll tell you what, the next time you try to get into my house you better have backup."

"You don't have a chance of stopping me, and I warn you I'm going to get what I want even if it's over your dead body," Randle threatened.

"Get away from me, you son of a bitch. You will get nothing from me except a trip to the morgue."

"Yeah, sure, like I said I'm frightened," Randle said

sarcastically, then, "I'll give you a little time to think things over. But the next time we talk you will give me the information I want, willingly or otherwise. See you around." He stalked off with confidence, knowing he had made his point to someone in a vulnerable position.

Sam hurriedly left the restaurant and on the way home started to devise a plan for dealing with Randle. After getting home, she went to the computer and began organizing things so that if anything were to happen to her, her affairs would be in order. No one would be able to access the inner workings of the murder-for-hire machinations—contacts, mysteriously interrelated money accounts, security codes, dead drop procedures etc. Josh had made it easy for her to destroy confidential data in an emergency. When activated by a special code that Sam was to create, the file would scrub the disc clean of everything outsiders should not see. Next she created a file which granted ownership of all business interests and all bank accounts to the person she most trusted in the world to carry out her wishes were she to be killed. The file could only be activated by the name of the person that was entered following it. All of this was in addition to the life insurance documentation that she had prepared right after her parents were killed as defense against the Wolf family.

The next day Sam spent several hours with her lawyer and business advisor to create the documents which would spell out the procedures for transferring all of her assets to the person she had designated as her executor and into whose hands she had entrusted her files. She followed up this effort with selected changes to the security system in her house.

# *Chapter Eighteen*

Sam had just returned from grocery shopping and was putting things away when the doorbell rang. She was aggravated about the interruption as she opened the door to find a rather disheveled Charles staring her in the face.

"Hello Sam it's nice to see you again after all this time."

Sam was startled and had to fight the impulse to close the door and thus shut out the disturbing past. After a long pause she finally replied in an annoyed tone one would use with a persistent bill collector, "Hello Charles, what are you doing here? We finished our conversation some time ago."

"But now I know what a mistake that was. My life has been a big muddle ever since," Charles blurted out. "Can I come in? I've got something very important I need to tell you."

"There's nothing to say Charles. You made it clear long ago how you felt. There's really no point to opening old wounds. I worked hard to forget you, and now I'd rather leave it that way."

"Please Sam, I was stupid and I've got to get something off my chest. You have reason to feel the way you do and I'll understand once you hear what I have to say, if you throw me out and write me off. But, I need to talk to you to clear the air. Please let me do that."

Silently she stared at the man she once loved and wondered if some remnant of that person still remained in this seemingly faded facsimile before her. After a few moments her curiosity got the better of her and she relented. "OK Charles, you can talk while I put away the groceries. Make it quick."

"Thank you Sam. I promise you won't regret this," he said as he followed her into the house.

Walking into the kitchen Sam felt great trepidation about her decision to let Charles in, but she turned and said, "You look like you could use something to drink."

"Yeah, thanks, I could use some water."

After Sam poured a glass of ice water, they sat for a long time in silence at the kitchen table staring at each other trying to see inside the each other. Charles tried to clear his thoughts, dry his moist eyes, and gain control of his voice. Sam could see that Charles was very anxious about something and it made her uncomfortable. She hoped that she would not regret her decision to let him come into the house.

Charles finally said, "Sam this whole experience of being with you again is so special I can't adequately deal with the emotions that I'm feeling. It's very difficult to find the words to express myself without bursting out in tears."

"I'm surprised, you're usually so good with words." Sam chided.

"The last time I felt complete was the last time we were

together before all the shooting started.  After that, one thing led to another and I just lost it."

"So I've heard," Sam said with no emotion.

"First I stupidly withdrew from you. Then I compounded that, after being shot, by turning to liquor and pills.  My mind was in disarray and my body was broken. I was unable to make good decisions and I made a lot of bad ones."

Sam finally felt some sympathy for this apparently fractured person.  "I really don't know what you have in mind Charles, but there is no way that I can come back into your life. So much has happened that I couldn't find my way back to that place."

"Yes, I know.  That's more than I have a right to expect." Sam's caring tone gave Charles confidence as he spoke. "During the past year I have often sifted through what my life has become, and deeply longed for the good things that I let slip through my fingers in the past."

"That's not unusual, I do that all the time."

"Yes but you were the part of my life that was the most cherished, and the one whose loss I regret because it was for such a selfish reason."

"Charles please! I don't need to hear this. What I thought we had was an illusion, I understand that and have moved on."

"No, I'm being honest for the first time in a long time. I need to tell you something important, just like the time you opened your heart to me."

"Being truthful will only get you hurt. I learned that the hard way."

"I know but I'm willing to suffer the consequence just as you were. I only hope that you can be more compassionate than I was."

"Charles, you're being melodramatic. And it's not necessary you…"

"Yes, Sam it is necessary." Charles felt compelled to proceed with his mission and he assertively interrupted Sam. "It will bring closure for both of us. It has to do with Josh and why he died."

At the mention of Josh's name Sam was sure she was wrong to have let this stranger into her house. "How would you know anything about Josh?"

"Well I…"

"Whatever you have to say, I don't want to hear it," Sam interrupted.

"I've got to…"

"Please don't do this!" She rose from her chair and backed away from the table. She didn't want to hear what she knew was coming.

Charles ignored her actions and insistently continued, "It's been too long Sam, and the secret has nearly destroyed us both." He paused briefly and then blurted out, "My father and I are responsible for Josh's death."

"That's ridiculous," Sam shouted. "I don't believe you."

"You've got to believe it, Sam. As terrible as it sounds, dad and I took out the original contract to have Chandler killed, then we paid to have your husband killed after he killed Carolyn by mistake."

Sam threw her hands over her face and began to sob. "Oh my god—no!"

"I know Sam, it's repugnant and painful. But when your husband shot Mr. Chandler and the bullet also killed Carolyn, my father and I went completely nuts, and had Josh killed in a fit of rage. As far as we were concerned, his screw up was irredeemable. He was supposed to do a clean hit but instead he killed Carolyn and we just went crazy with hatred and shame."

"Charles you bastard! You and your father were supposed to be pillars of virtue not murderers!" Sam shouted at him.

"I know, that's what makes our actions so shameful and disgusting. I tried to hide behind the booze and pills so that I didn't have to take responsibility. Finally I knew I had to tell you no matter what."

Sam stood in silence and intensely searched Charles' face and her own emotions. She strolled aimlessly around the kitchen before she moved to the sink and splashed her face with cold water, then filled a glass.

"If you want to get your gun and take revenge, I understand. I won't defend myself," Charles assured her.

She fingered the thigh strap that held her gun and stared at her reflection in the window over the sink as she took a sip of water.

She then resumed her silent walk around the kitchen, repeatedly circling Charles as a hungry tiger might circle an incapacitated prey. They both knew that Sam could strike at any moment and that knowledge created intense emotion in both stalker and prey. Finally she sat down and continued staring at Charles. He sat silently awaiting his execution.

Finally Sam spoke with an unsteady voice, "I knew that you could be responsible for Josh's death, but I never believed it was true. I always thought that it had to be someone else. It just didn't seem possible that you or your dad would do something like that."

"I felt the same way," Charles admitted. "After the fact I felt disgusted and terribly remorseful. I couldn't stand myself."

"Now that I know the truth I ache for revenge just like I would if it had been any miscreant on the street," Sam said with unabridged contempt.

They sat in silence for several minutes just staring at each other, then Charles said in a soft, passive voice that bespoke his self loafing, "If you feel that you want to take your revenge, I'll give you time to get your gun. Death may relieve the pain caused by the dreadful hate I have for myself."

"Your death would be good for both of us."

"I never stopped loving you Sam. I want you to know that."

After more silence and intense introspection, Sam said, "Part of me wants not only you, but your entire family stacked in a pile and set afire just as Josh was."

Charles was startled by the harshness of Sam's words and begged, "No, Sam. This is not about my family; it's only about me. I'm the one you should hold responsible. Just leave what's left of my family out of this. I have already lost the person I loved best in my family. I live every day with the agony of Carolyn's death, knowing I was responsible."

"You deserve to lose everything that's dear to you. You don't get to choose."

Charles was covered in sweat as he replied resolutely, "You've got to do what you've got to do."

Sam watched her victim squirm as she continued to weigh her options, and after several minutes she took the gun from her thigh holster and placed it on the table. After several more minutes Sam picked up the gun and pointed it at Charles' head and she slowly put pressure on the trigger. Charles made a whimpering sound as he prepared to die.

After an agonizing moment Sam abruptly released her finger and slammed the gun on the table, stood up and moved away from the table giving Charles plenty of time to pick it up and protect himself. He stared alternately between Sam and her gun, but remained motionless. She then came back to the table, picked up the gun and circled Charles several more times as she fingered the gun and pondered the situation. Finally she again threw the gun to the table and furiously pounded the table with both hands as she screamed, "God damn you Charles, I just can't do it. I can not pull the damn trigger."

Sam's words astounded Charles. He sat with his heart pounding and sweat rolling down his forehead, as he tried to internalize his new fate. "When I came here I was prepared to die; in fact I thought I should die," he said slowly. "But that was not my decision to make. I hope you are doing the right thing for both of us."

"The role I played in this ugly mess won't allow me to continue the carnage Charles. But I don't think I can ever forgive you for initiating this entire mess."

"I understand. It's too much to ask for your forgiveness; a lack of vengeance is the most I could hope for."

"Why on earth did I let you in today?"

"Maybe it was providence. Mustering up the strength to tell you about Josh was something I had to do; your reaction confirms that. Now I have to wrap my mind around the possibility that I might leave here in one piece with the chance to put my screwed up life back together."

Sam tried to explain her lack of appetite for revenge. "Josh and I were responsible for Mr. Chandler's and Carolyn's deaths just as much as you were. I didn't pull the trigger, but I was there.  I saw it happen, and I feel responsible for the pain that their deaths caused the Chandler and Bennington families.  Part of me feels like I should be seeking your forgiveness, I think that's why I can't pull the trigger now."

After reflecting on Sam's explanation Charles confided, "When you first told me about your background, you had no way of knowing, of course, that I knew the whole story."

"What do you mean the whole story?"

"When you told me about your husband being a hit man that was killed and burned in a barrel in Cancun, I knew that dad and I were responsible for his death.  It just staggered me."

"You didn't let on, I was completely unaware."

"We were afraid that you knew that we were the ones who had hired Josh and that you had come back to Crown City to take revenge on us.  That's why I had to distance myself from you even though it broke my heart."

"When you threw me over I wished that you had just killed me.  It would have been less painful."

"I understand the pain because I was truly in love with you Sam."

"Since Josh was killed, my emotions have taken me on a Ferris wheel ride, sending me into fits of ecstasy or depression for no reason," Sam confided.

"By the time you came to Crown City I had taken out

my anger on Josh for Carolyn's death and I couldn't extend it to you."

"People do strange things sometimes. I hope you can forgive me for my role in all this."

"I do forgive you for your part in Carolyn's death, if that helps you in some way. It doesn't amount to much, compared to what you have given me today."

"I really haven't done anything today but control my anger. You have gained whatever strength you have on your own."

"You gave me plenty Sam. I came here prepared to die and you let me live. I've got a lot of broken fences to mend but at lease now there will be a tomorrow in which to do it."

"It took courage for you to tell me about your responsibility for Josh's death and I think you feel better having made that confession. You seem to have dug yourself out of a pile of crap, and in so doing helped me smell a little better as well."

"There was a time when I thought I was something special. I was a Bennington, after all. But when I was forced to deliver on my own, under pressure, I completely blew apart."

Each of them could feel the emotional tensions between them dissipating, and when Sam spoke she was more at ease. "It's sometimes hard to get how you think of yourself to match reality, but when they come together it usually brings you peace of mind."

"But, you know, in the long run it probably doesn't make a hill of beans how powerful a person thinks he is," Charles asserted. "Life is a giant river that keeps to its course and performs as nature intended. It doesn't remember any individual no matter how big he thought he was."

Sam was surprised by Charles philosophical words because that was so atypical of the "old Charles" and she smiled as she said, "Great thoughts, but strange words coming from you. Have you become the philosopher now?"

Charles laughed, "You taught me to think that way and it's the only thing that brought me out of the wilderness."

Encouraged by the changed mood, Sam filled two glasses of wine from a previously opened bottle. "Maybe there's hope for you after all, Charles."

Charles laughed and said, "I surely hope so and I owe it all to you. We could go on all night confessing our sins, but I don't think there is much more to be accomplished."

"No but strangely I do feel better inside," Sam mused.

They peered into each other's eyes as they tapped glasses, took a sip of wine and reflected on what had been said; acknowledging the comfort that comes from understanding something important. They each appreciated having a companion in that awareness and it rekindled emotions they thought had been lost. There was a bit of skepticism mixed with hope for a return to happier times together.

The kitchen door being thrown open and slammed against the wall with a crashing sound shattered their tranquility. Startled, Sam and Charles turned to find Ralph Randle standing in the doorway with a gun in his hand, "Well, well, how touching."

"Randle, what the hell are you doing here? I told you to get lost," Sam shouted.

"Yeah and I believe you meant it. So I decided to do things my way and force you to do what I want. Finding this jerk here is a bonus. I can get rid of him if I have to and make it look like it was a lovers' quarrel, and nobody will be the wiser."

"Look Randle, leave Charles out of this. There is no reason to involve him."

"Well, maybe I was being a bit hasty," Randle chided. "All you have to do is give me the information I need, and everyone gets out of here alive."

"I can't do that Randle, you know that. The system just won't allow it."

"Well I'm fixing to change the system. I think I'm smart enough to make it work a new way. Now step over here little man before I blow your head off."

"Look, Randle, I have compiled everything I know about the Wolf family and if I'm killed all that information will be sent to the authorities automatically. If you hurt me it will bring down the Wolf family. Is that what you want?"

"I don't care about the Wolf family. They haven't done squat for me."

"Are you trying to tell me that you're not acting on behalf of the Wolfs?"

"I told you that before; now let's get on with our business."

Charles, with wide eyes and an anxious voice exclaimed, "Sam what is he talking about? Are you in some sort of trouble?"

"No Charles, it's just a business misunderstanding. Why don't you just leave? I can handle this."

"Oh he's not going anywhere. First I'm going to shoot him in one leg, then ask you for the information. If you don't cooperate I'll shoot him in the other leg, and so on until I blow his brains out. Then I'll take care of you in the same way. Now why don't you be a good girl and do as I want so this prissy uptight blue-blooded snob doesn't get hurt?"

"Please Randle, leave Charles out of this. You know I can't give you the information you want. I'm the only one who can conduct our business. That's just the way things are."

"Well we can just set things up differently, with me in charge. Now tell me what I need to know or this guy loses a leg!"

"Look here mister, I won't let you hurt Sam!" With that Charles hurled himself at Randle in an attempt to wrestle the gun away. Sidestepping, Randle fired a shot at Charles hitting him in the chest. Bright red began spreading on the front of his shirt as Charles fell to the floor. Sam used that split second to retrieve her gun from the table and aim. Simultaneous shots rang out and each antagonist fell to the floor; Randle with a bullet hole in his forehead and Sam with one in her gut. Dazed and oozing blood Sam hit the panic button on her cell phone for Chief Watson and 911. Her head then drooped to the floor and her world became dark.

***

Sam regained consciousness after a few moments and she wadded up some of her skirt and held it tightly against the wound in the right side of her abdomen. She tried to relax and conserve energy when she heard the sirens outside.

Chief Watson was the first to enter the house. He found Randle dead. Charles was unconscious and bleeding but still alive. Sam had lost a lot of blood, but was still holding on.

The Chief carefully put his arm under Sam's neck and raised her head slightly. The part of the skirt that Sam held tightly against her wound was now soaked in blood, and he helped her replace it with a fresh piece. He then whispered, "Sam, what happened?"

Sam coughed a couple of times and then said, "Charles and I were here talking, trying to understand the past when Randle broke in. He waved his gun around and threatened to shoot us both." She coughed again, took a deep breath and said, "Charles was trying to save me when Randle shot him.  He was just putting his life back together and I got him killed."  Sam spoke with an ever-weakening voice.

"He's still alive Sam, he's got a chance to make it." Chief Watson responded.

"While Randle was threatening us he bragged about killing Chandler and Carolyn as well as my husband. He said he was trying to establish himself as a big time hit man," Sam lied.

"He told you that?"

"That's what he said so help me."  Sam continued her fabrications, "And he was proud of it.  Turns out the Wolf's had nothing to do with any of the stuff going on in town.  Mr. Wolf went after me because he thought I had something to do with his son's death, but now that's cleared up."

"You may be right about that, but let's get you to the hospital now.  How badly are you hurt?"

"It's pretty bad, I'm getting light headed," Sam said in a weak faltering voice.

"Just hang on, OK?"

"I'll try James, but death is not always a bad thing; good things often follow someone's passing."

"Can't let that happen until I find out who you really are," he assured her.

"Don't work too hard at it James.  I'm not the person I was…I'm not the person I became…and I'm not the person I will become.  You'll have to hit a moving target and I'm not really worth it."

The paramedics pushed the Chief aside; pressure dressed Sam's wound, started an IV, then rolled her onto a stretcher and made their way to the ambulance.

Chief Watson followed and asked, "Is she going to make it?"

"She's lost a lot of blood, but she'll pull through."

"What about Mr. Bennington and the other guy?"

"One's a goner but I'm not sure about the other."

****

Sam was in the OR for five hours to repair her wounds. The next afternoon when she had been awake and alert for a couple of hours she asked the nurse in her private room to bring her a phone and give her some privacy. Struggling, at times to catch her breath she dialed the phone.  When the party answered she said in a weak voice, "Hello Walter."

"Hello Sam, I'm glad you're feeling well enough to call."

"Thanks, I just needed to tell you that I did what I said I would do; Randle is dead."

"When I first learned that Randle was the one who killed Josh we had to retaliate I know you understand

240

that," Mr. Wolf replied. "It pleased me that you agreed to take him out when I called you the other day to tell you about Randle's involvement. Now the circle is closed."

"I agree it had to be done Walter, as it turned out I was just defending myself, which made it easier for me."

"I know it was tough for you Sam, you never really bought into the family business."

"I must admit there was some satisfaction in killing the guy who burned up Josh. But it will take some time for me to get over Charles being shot again."

"How did that go down?"

"Charles came to my house to confess that he and his dad paid to have Josh killed. I was furious and wanted desperately to shoot him, but when it came right down to it I just couldn't pull the trigger. While Charles and I were talking Randle broke into the house and waved his gun around. Charles rushed him and during the scuffle, Randle shot him, I shot Randle, and he got me on the way down."

"So Randle shot Bennington huh, there's a certain irony in that."

"Another irony is that I never killed anyone until I came to Crown City trying to get away from you. Strange world, huh?"

"I'll say. Anyway, I guess this puts things to rest. I'm no longer holding you responsible for Josh's death."

"Gee thanks, but really I can't blame you for suspecting

me Walter, it's a terrible thing to lose your only son that way."

"Just so you know, the snitch who gave up Randle also gave up the Benningtons," Mr. Wolf replied. "We were going to take them both out because we knew it would be hard for you, but we couldn't find the son. Now I know why, he was with you. We got the father earlier in the day. It may look like Randle did that too, if we're lucky."

"It's a sad day in Crown City, losing one prominent citizen and having his son still in intensive care not expected to live."

"I'll send my guy to the hospital and put an end to it," Mr. Wolf said.

"No I don't want you to do that," Sam interrupted. "If he dies that's one thing. But if he pulls through he has been through enough."

"He was responsible for Josh's death, he's got to go," Mr. Wolf blustered.

"Look, it was his father who bought the contract on Josh, not Charles. Besides we killed his sister and he has been shot twice, that should be enough."

"I don't know Sam, we should clean the plate."

"Let me decide how to handle it. If he dies, case closed. If not I'll take care of things, ok?"

"I hate to leave loose ends but I guess I can leave it in your hands."

"By the way where are you now Walter?"

"I came back to Chicago shortly after our little skirmish at the Country Club so that I couldn't be blamed for anything that happened there.  I left a guy to follow up on things."

"Very clever."

"Your taking out Randle was proof of your loyalty Sam. So you can walk away, if that's what you want, it's your choice.  That's an option no one's had before and I don't intend to offer it again."

"Do I have your word that you will cut me free—no strings—Walter?"

"Yeah, you don't have to look over your shoulder any more," Mr. Wolf promised.  "Besides you have that life insurance policy, as you call it."

"Yes there is that," Sam said cheerfully.  "I wonder what to do with it?"

"Keep it. Who knows, it may come in handy sometime," Mr. Wolf laughed.  "You plan to stay in Crown City?"

"I don't know yet.  I have to convince everyone here that I acted in self-defense and that I didn't have anything to do with the Chandler murder," Sam observed.  "Then there's the issue about my real identity.  I may have to move down south to be near Uncle Ernie and take back my real name. To bad, cause I really like being Sara Andre Mathews.  But the first thing I have to do is recover from the bullet hole in my gut."

"How bad is it?"

"It's bad enough to be concerned…the bullet may have nicked a lung…but I'm going to make it I think."

"Is there anything I can do for you?"

"I think I'm doing ok, Walter.  I'll send you a Christmas card."

"Hey, good luck in your new life, I don't expect to hear from you again."

"That is music to my ears sir…adieu."

# *Chapter Nineteen*

Charles and Sam sat on the back deck of his house overlooking the pool having coffee, juice and a roll while reading the morning paper as they often did since being discharged from the hospital.  They only visited her home to make sure the caretakers were doing their job and to pick up the mail; they were still not comfortable spending much time there.

"You know Sam we have been rehabbing from the shootings for almost three months now and nothing else," Charles said looking up and admiring the landscape, then finally continuing "I've been doing some serious thinking."

"Good for you Charles, you know what they say, "use it or lose it," Sam said smiling as she put aside the paper.

"Exactly!" Charles exclaimed.

"Exactly what?"

"Use it or lose it.  If we don't start doing something useful we could fossilize and be carted away to a museum or something.  We should be doing something."

"We are; we're reading the paper and having breakfast." Sam said unconcerned.

"I feel like we're wasting precious time.  We did some very scary things there for a while but at least we were doing something."

"Well as we demonstrated, just doing something is not necessarily a good thing," Sam shrugged.

"Yeah but I'm feeling pretty good now and maybe it's time to do something again, something worthwhile this time."

"So you think we should do something," Sam replied, still just barely interested in the conversation.

"Exactly."

"There you go again."

"Don't you feel we should be doing something other than working on our physical condition?"

"It's kind of fun doing nothing."

"Yeah I know but now it's time to do something."

"If you say that one more time I'll brain you."

"Ok, ok."

"I do have an idea though; it's been percolating for awhile actually."

"What?"

"It has to do with the Chandlers."

"Oh god I don't know…the Chandlers?"

"Yeah, the Chandlers. Mr. Chandler sort of brought us together in a ghoulish way. Maybe Mrs. Chandler can lead us out of our funk."

"What do you have in mind?"

"Last I heard, the Chandler Building was still on the market.  Perhaps we could take it off Mrs. Chandler's hands and restore it, like we once started...before you went crazy."

"Wouldn't that be something," Charles said with a sense of wonder.

"It would hardly make up for Mr. Chandler's demise, but it could help Pauline and maybe us as well," Sam suggested.

Charles put his chin in his hands and shook his head, "I get the creeps when I think about what Dad and I did to the Chandlers."

"Neither one of us pulled the trigger, but we are both guilty in a way.  That will always be with us."

They both sat in silence for a long time before Charles said, "The Chandler Building, huh?"  That was followed by a much longer silence.

"Maybe we should give Mrs. Chandler a call and see how she feels about it," Sam said finally breaking the silence.  "What do you think?"

"I don't know Sam, this is serious stuff.  Restoring the Chandler building will take a lot of time and money."

"It would be a challenge Charles; that's what you were looking for, right?"

Still with a puzzled look on his face Charles said, "Ok, why don't you give her a call?"

Before she got cold feet Sam picked up the phone and dialed. "Hello Mrs. Chandler, this is Sam Mathews, remember me?" Sam said as she tightly pressed the receiver to her ear.

After a moment of silence Mrs. Chandler said, "Of course my dear. It's been a long time since we last spoke."

"The reason I'm calling is that Charles and I were reminiscing and began talking about you and the Chandler Building, and wondered if it had been sold."

"Nothing has changed, its still sitting there empty, kind of like my life right now."

"Oh good…I mean about the building. I'm sorry that you're feeling depressed. Maybe we can help each other by renewing our plan to restore the old lady…the building I mean. Sorry. Well, you know what I mean."

"I know what you mean Sam, don't worry. By 'we' you mean you and Charles, I assume."

"Yes, Charles. We would do it as a joint venture, just as we planned to do before everything unraveled."

"Is your intended partnership just professional or is there more to it now."

"It's a pretty tight bond right now Pauline, but who really knows about things like that?"

"It's funny how things sometimes happen in parallel. You kids have been on my mind lately. I was wondering what you were doing, but I was hesitant to call."

"Great!  How about joining us on Charles's yacht for a day trip to Catalina?  It would give us a chance to catch up on things and talk about the future. What do you think?"

"I think that might work.  I'm happy to hear that you're back together.  There was much to bind you."

"We can go any day this week; your pick."

"Give me a couple of days to settle my schedule," Mrs. Chandler cheerfully exclaimed.

"Then it's set.  We'll pick you up early Wednesday.  I know we'll have a great time.  Bye Pauline."

After hanging up the phone Sam turned to Charles, "I'm really looking forward to talking with Pauline, she was always so supportive of me when you were such a shit."

"That wasn't the real me."

"I know," Sam said soothingly.

****

Charles made arrangements with his crew to make the yacht ready for Wednesday morning.  They picked up Pauline and made their way by car to Newport Beach where his yacht was moored.  Once on board they made themselves comfortable as the crew prepared the craft and set out for Catalina. Upon leaving the harbor Charles returned from the galley with drinks for the three of them.

Once seated Charles turned to Mrs. Chandler, "We have had a long and difficult history Pauline," and holding up his glass he continued, "here's to forgetting the past and starting anew."

Charles toast was followed by "I'll drink to that" in unison as they enjoyed the ice cold Chardonnay.

After a silence and a couple of sips of wine Pauline said, "Charles this is such a lovely day. Thank you for the invitation."

"Don't mention it. Looking back, the feud between our families was stupid. Life is too short for things like that. I'm just sorry that dad couldn't be here with us."

"Your father was a good man, Charles."

"He had his moments I guess."

"The feud was always between he and my husband. Did he ever have a heart to heart with you about the reasons?"

"No not really, all he did since I can remember was call Osborn names and tell me what a bad guy he was. He never said why he felt that way. I just thought it was because they were in constant business competition. I didn't know how personal it was until the end."

"Yes it was very personal and I was caught up in the middle of it."

"Oh really, how?" Charles inquired.

"I really don't know that I should get into the details, it

would probably only muddy the water."

"The suspense is killing me; how were you in the middle of the feud?"

"Oh I don't know Charles."

"Dad never said a bad word about you, he always had flattering words for you and how sad he was that you were married to such a bum."

"I often thought of Osborn that way too; but I shouldn't get into this," Pauline said with a worried look on her face as if she had opened a can of worms and didn't know how to put the lid back on.

"I don't want to make you uncomfortable but I really would like to know more about it."

"Oh Charles," Pauline said as she reached for and gently held his hand in hers and thoughtfully examined his face. "I have never regarded you as an enemy. Never."

"That's nice to hear Pauline. For me it was always Osborn who was the bad guy not you."

She paused for several minutes before continuing. "Your father, Osborn and I were friends throughout high school and college."

"What was it that drove Dad and Osborn apart?"

"Actually I was dating your father for most of the time we were in school and we went on many double dates with Osborn and several other girls."

"Really?"

"During the last two years of college your dad and I talked seriously about getting married."

"You're kidding," Charles said releasing Pauline's hand. "I wonder why he didn't tell me that?"

"I shouldn't say any more. Really Charles, let's just drop the subject, ok? It's a lovely day," Pauline said, as her eyes became watery and her voice began to waver.

"I really would like to know what happened Pauline, but if the memories are difficult for you I understand."

"Oh Charles it's so hard," she said as she turned and dried her eyes with her napkin.

After sitting silently listening with great interest Sam reached out to Charles and said, "Please Charles maybe it would be best to continue this later when Pauline has gathered herself."

"Yes, yes of course," Charles reluctantly concurred.

After sitting in silence for several minutes Pauline said with still watery eyes, "Now that I have come this far it would be unfair not to tell you everything. I've wanted to for so many years but I just didn't have the courage."

"I very much want to hear about you and dad, but I don't want you to feel uncomfortable."

"I should have done this a long time ago," she said and then paused before continuing. "Just before graduation, your dad and I went to his parents and told them of our plans to marry." She again paused to gather her thoughts.

"The two of you were thinking of marriage?"

"Your grandparents were just horrified that your dad would pick a girl without the proper background, it would just not do."

"That figures."

"They had already picked out the proper girl in the proper family and that's the way it would have to be. Your dad went ballistic, screamed and yelled but in the end the Bennington family won out as usual."

"Damn the Bennington family, no wonder dad and I were so screwed up. I hate the Bennington family sometimes." He slipped his arm around Pauline and pulled her close to him. Sam joined their emotional release and tears flowed all around.

After some time Pauline continued, "I was devastated at the rejection and I think went a little crazy. Osborn was very supportive and got me through the toughest time. I was so grateful to him that when he suggested it, we just ran off and got married. Stupid behavior of course, but young people aren't very rational at times like that. A few months later along came a baby. Osborn could count very well and he knew he could not be the father of the child and that's how it all started."

"Oh my god your son Albert is actually my half brother," Charles exclaimed to the sky as he heavily sat back in his chair.

The three of them sat and stared at each other until Sam finally summarized, "Wow you guys are practically family."

"I guess you could say that. It's how I've always felt," Pauline admitted. "In fact Charles, your father and I have talked from time to time over the years."

"Is that a fact?" Charles exclaimed.

"He even admitted that he was responsible for Osborn's death and how all that played out, including your husband's involvement, Sam."

"You knew all that and didn't say anything," Sam said showing great surprise. "You are some strong lady."

"Good lord what a threesome we turned out to be," added Charles with a dumbfounded look on his face. He then continued to refill their glasses with wine and they silently drank and thought about the latest turn of events until the bottle was empty.

Finally Pauline rose to make a statement, "I have thought long and hard about the role each of you played in Osborn's death. At first I was in great pain and I wanted to repay you in kind. But in time the pain lessened and I came to more fully realize there is a drastic difference between the physical act that causes death and that of just being associated with the perpetrator. A coconspirator is not blameless and their actions do need retribution. But the level of punishment should be tailored to the degree of their participation and their character and actions following the crime. I now believe that both of you have demonstrated to my satisfaction that you deserve special treatment and that it would please me to participate in your retribution. So I would like to propose that we form a partnership to rehabilitate the Chandler Building together and when it is completed we rename it The Redemption Building. It can then stand for the rest of our lives as a reminder of what was done and as atonement for our part in it. You have already paid a price in your lives for what was done and little else needs to be done to square yourselves with society or with me. What do ya think?"

Sam and Charles sat silently staring at each other and Pauline for several minutes before Sam said, "You are a very wise and charitable friend Pauline."

Charles then raised his glass and said, "Here's to the Crown City Redemption." They all raised their glasses in jubilant concurrence.

After several minutes, Sam's face turned solemn and, smelling the air she turned to Charles, "What is that smell…gas or something?"

Charles took a couple of whiffs and said, "I had some galley work done last week maybe there's a propane leak. That's what it smells like." Just as he got up to take a look a huge explosion shattered the hull and buckled the deck sending several pieces catapulting into the air along with the three "partners."

Sam felt a profound feeling of falling and eventually found herself several feet below the water's surface. Instinct protects one under those circumstances and she held her breath as she oriented herself and made her way to the surface with flailing arms and legs. Upon reaching the surface she coughed out the water in her mouth and throat and took several gulps of air as she scanned the wreckage spread over several yards of ocean. She spied a flotation ring and swam to it as she continued her search of the water's surface for any sign of Charles or Pauline.

Suddenly she caught sight of a hand peeking through the water several feet away. Next came some gray hair and then Pauline's head spitting and sputtering uncontrollably. Then she disappeared. Sam slid one arm through the floats rope and began swimming toward where she had seen Pauline.

Sam searched the surface with no success and then she took a deep breath and plunged under water to continue her search. She looked frantically in all directions but found nothing. She ran out of air and returned to the surface thinking that it was probably already too late to find Pauline alive, but she made one more under water search. Her lungs were about to burst when she saw through the murky water a shadowy figure. She swam to the object and determined that it was indeed Pauline; she was not moving. Sam grabbed the collar of Paulines jacket and kicked and thrashed her way to the surface. She could see that Pauline was not breathing and quickly swam to the float while holding Pauline's face above water.

Life and death are difficult concepts to characterize under the best of circumstances and sometimes it's difficult to distinguish them during the time of crossover.

In the struggle between the forces, life must completely surrender before death can rule. Sam had to believe that life's surrender came grudgingly and that Pauline still retained that tiny spark which if properly fanned could rekindle the depleted forces of life.

Sam slapped Pauline's face several times as she implored her to "wake up" and "come back to me." She then grabbed Pauline's nose and blew into her mouth all the while struggling to keep the two of them afloat. Crying uncontrollably, for reasons she didn't completely understand she could barely get a full breath into Pauline's lungs. Her first effort had no affect and she hurriedly blew again, but still Pauline did not respond. She then began pounding Pauline's chest with her fist making a last desperate attempt to dislodge deaths grip.

After three additional lungs full and continued pounding, a volume of water and air was expelled from Pauline's lungs and she began ferociously coughing and gasping for air as she struggled to escape Sam's unrelenting assault. Sam fought to keep Pauline' head above water while rejecting Pauline's attempts to escape. She searched Pauline's face as tears streamed down her face and she screamed "Yes, yes, that's it, you got it, we won."

Sam's screaming and violent activity finally caught Charles' eye from some distance away. He swam toward them with his one good arm while dragging his re-injured arm (the same one that had been shot twice and now was painful and not correctly functioning).

He finally reached the two women as Pauline relaxed and said her first words, "Please Sam, don't hit me any more."

"I'm sorry Pauline, but I just couldn't let you go without a fight."

"I held my breath for as long as I could and then I gave up and sort of went to sleep."

"I was completely out of control," Sam admitted.

"Everything was peaceful for a while and then all of a sudden I was aware that you were hitting and screaming at me."

"Honestly, I felt like I was fighting death; determined to make it go away.  I never felt so strong," Sam said triumphantly.

Pauline continued, "I tried to protect myself from being attacked.  I think that's what woke me up."

"I didn't mean to hurt you but something just wouldn't let me give up on you."

"Thank you, I know you did it to save me."

"I'm just happy that we all made it," Charles chimed in.

The three of them held tightly to the float and each other for several minutes.  Finally a rescue boat pulled up along side them and two rescuers entered the water to help everyone to safety.  On board Pauline was administered oxygen and treated for the cuts and bruises inflicted by the explosion and Sam's assault.  They all were covered with heated blankets and provided hot coffee.

Upon becoming more comfortable Pauline quipped, "Is it too late to back out of our partnership.  I think I might be too old for all this excitement."

"Yes it's too late, it's a done deal," Charles said as he reached out to hold her hand.

"I guess you're stuck with us Pauline, no matter what," Sam said as she leaned over and kissed her on the cheek.

On the way to shore the three of them held snugly together signifying that indeed a lasting, if unlikely, partnership had been forged.

# *The End*

www.ingramcontent.com/pod-product-compliance
Lightning Source LLC
Chambersburg PA
CBHW070917190726
48292CB00004B/1006